The Big Green Poetry Machine

Poems From Across The UK

Edited by Lisa Adlam

First published in Great Britain in 2009 by:

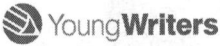

Young Writers
Young Writers
Remus House
Coltsfoot Drive
Peterborough
PE2 9JX
Telephone: 01733 890066
Website: www.youngwriters.co.uk

All Rights Reserved
Book Design by Spencer Hart & Tim Christian
© Copyright Contributors 2008
SB ISBN 978-1-84924-068-0

Foreword

Young Writers' Big Green Poetry Machine is a showcase for our nation's most brilliant young poets to share their thoughts, hopes and fears for the planet they call home.

Young Writers was established in 1991 to nurture creativity in our children and young adults, to give them an interest in poetry and an outlet to express themselves. Seeing their work in print will encourage them to keep writing as they grow, and become our poets of tomorrow.

Selecting the poems has been challenging and immensely rewarding. The effort and imagination invested by these young writers makes their poems a pleasure to enjoy reading time and time again.

Contents

Alcott Hall Primary School, Solihull
Bethany Ball (7) 1

Barlestone CE Primary School, Barlestone
Luke Boonham (11) 1
Becky Harvey (10), Daisy Forman,
Eve & Megan 2
Emma Groves & Miranda Ratcliffe (10) 2
Katie Poole & Ashleigh Statham (10) 3
Courtney Marie Jones (10) 3
Thomas Cooper & Ashley Cooper (11) 4
Billy Mugglestone (10) & Macorley 4

Castlecombe Primary School, Mottingham
Cally Smith (8) 5
Emma Coyne 5
Anya Wood (8) 6
Gracie Davies-Whitehair 6
Olivia Smithson 7
Samantha-Jaine Ellis 7
Jessie Megan Elliott 8
Shannon Hyde (9) 8
Leah Musto (9) 9
Chelsea Thomas 9
Alfie Tilley (8) 10
Emily Cox (9) 10
Nathan Conroy (8) 11
James Dilley (8) 11
Pedro Spinola (7) 12
Jamie Chipping (8) 12
Alfie Mackinnon 13
Rachel Nash (8) 13
Millie Norton 14

Chennestone Primary School, Sunbury
Class 6G (10-11) 14
Class 3W (7-8) 15
Class 6B (10-11) 16

Class 4F (8-9) 17
Class 3A (7-8) 18

Congerstone Primary School, Congerstone
George Welton (11) 18
Emma Kelwin (10) 19
Ellie Jane Lawrence (11) 20
Jasmine Towersey (9) 21
Emily-Jayne Marston (9) 22
Thomas Paice (10) 23
Liberty Jackson (10) 24
Rheo Parnell (9) 25
Victoria Riley (10) 26
Clarice May Benney (9) 27
Kai Tannicliffe (9) 28
Jack Collin (10) 29
Leah Rutley (10) 30
Sam Bridle (9), Finn Campton
& Owen Blythe (10) 31
Harriet Moss (11) 31
Daisy Handford (10) 32
Ryan Gordon (9) 32
Niamh Harriman (10) 33
Will Abell (10) 33
Kitty Handford (9) 34
Morgan Lock (9) 34
Catherine Abell (8) 35
Charlotte Vasey (10) 35
Harry Talbot (10) 36
Josh Cumbley (11) 36
Sophie Wilkins (8) 37
Joshua Jones (10) 37
Bradley McLean (10) 38
Mackenzie Moore (9) 38
Joshua Munroe (8) 39
Harry Payne (11) 39
George Holmes (10) 40

Dragon School, Oxford

Alec Deakin (7) 40
Orlando Riviere (7) 41
Cian Ellis (7) 41
Flora Smiley (8) 42
Henry Williams (8) 42
Tiggy Greenfield (8) 43
Alexander Bellenie (7) 43
Gus Cayzer (8) 44
Alec Michaelis (8) 44
Flora Frankopan (7) 45
Jacob Bright (8) & Rhodri Whiteley (7) ... 45
Amelia Whinney (7) 46
Joshua van der Merwe (7) 46
Jamie Volak (8) 47
Anthony Monaco 47
Luke Miles 47
Tom Willcox (7) 48
Annabel Cave (7) 48
Maya Stern (7) 48
Tom Mills (7) 49
Poppy Webb (7) 49
Alexandra Kosobucki (7) 49
Jenny Hannah (7) 50
Saskia Orr 50
Rose Rooney (7) 50
Charlotte Hope (7) 51
Jack Stacey (7) 51
Ollie Brown (7) 51
India Deakin (7) 52
Catherine Churchill (8) 52
Rachel Oldershaw (7) 52
Tom van Oss (8) 53
Lucy Hope (7) 53
Charlie Girelli-Kent (7) 53
Katia Theologis (7) 54
Maddie Campion (7) 54
Charlie McCammon (8) 54
Katarina Frankopan (7) 54
Katherine Cochrane (7) 55
Sebastian Ingham (7) 55
Harriet Harries-Jones (7) 55
Stella Cohen (7) 55
Emma Wheatland (7) 56

Elton CE Primary School, Elton

Marisa Orton (9) 56

Llancarfan Primary School, Llancarfan

Holly Nicholls (7) 57
Nicole Lawson (8) 57

Lutley Primary School, Halesowen

Laura Billingham (10) 58
Heather Pope (10) 59
Amber Barnsley (11) 60
Katie Wrighton (10) 61
Sophie Hughes (11) 62
George Wakeman (11) 63
Michael Eaton (10) 64
Lydia Hanson (10) 64
Megan Abbie Morris (10) 65
Samantha Rostron (10) 65
Roshni McCarthy (10) 66
Olivia Symes (10) 66
Ellie Bryan (11) 67
Agnes Ranford (10) 67
Sophie Griffiths (10) 68
Adam Baker (11) 68
Megan Willetts (11) 69
Daniel Jennings (10) 69
Laura Humphries (11) 70
Katie Parton (10) 70
Sam Jones (10) 71

Norton-in-Hales CE Primary School, Market Drayton

George Tavernor (9) 71
Bethany Horne (9) 72
Sorcha Neill (8) 72
Lewis McDonald (7) 73
Lydia Cliffe (8) 73
Jessica Tong (7) 73
Kitty Lambert (7) 74
Owen Lloyd (8) 74
James McClelland (8) 74
Henry Smith (8) 75
Eleanor Bradeley (8) 75
Mae Brennan (7) 75

Thomas Healey (7) 76
Connor Bentley (7) 76

Old Oak Primary School, London
Reece Gairy (10) 76
Ahmed Asad (10) 77
Kausar Saeedi (10) 78
Madlina Haziraj (10) 78
Asma Zaglam (10) 79
Kearnaye Dunn & Khadija Said (10) 79
Hammam Aboulfath (10) 80
Xenral Imiuru (9) 80
Moustafa Katamesh (10) 81
Ryan Jones (10) 81

Rogiet Primary School, Rogiet
Joshua Parr (10) 81
Lucy Jenkins 82
Josh Carron (9) 82
Sinead Little (9) 83
Connor Kington 83
Chloe Knight (9) 84
Sophie Powell (9) 84
Alice Davies (9) 85

St David's RC Primary School, Newport
Tonicha Luffman (10) 85
Regan Crockett (7) 86
Elisabeth Williams (10) 86
Hannah Price (10) 87
Bethan Davidge (10) 87
Grace Hurley (8) 88
Luc Taran Joseff Simmonds (8) 88
Jessica Nightingale (10) 89
Carys Parselle (8) 89
Megan Hughes (9) 89
Ffion Joseph (10) 90
William Ryley (10) 90
Ieuan Matthews (8) 90
Mollie Joseph (7) 91
Jordan Lois Ingles (8) 91
Niall Graham (8) 91
Georgia Hillman (9) 92
Kevin Sunil (8) 92
Elinor Davies (7) 92

Emily Friel (8) 93
Evie Bignell (8) 93
Erin Bryony Martin (7) 93
Sinead Davison (8) 94

St John's Primary School, Barrhead
Heather MacNeil 94
Chloe O'Hara 95
Caitlin Curran (10) 96
Erin Cassidy (8) 97
Holly Harris 98
Lauren McGuire (10) 99
Hannah Coyle 100
Jodie Robb (9) 100
Carly Bremner (10) 101
Jack Phillips (9) 102
Kevin Walsh (9) 102
Emily Docherty (10) 103
Kyle Johnston (10) 104
Rachel Hughes 105
Adam Canning (9) 106
Aidan McGuigan (9) 106
Erin Shankland (10) 107
Carmen Cassidy 107
Anna Campbell (9) 108

Shinewater Primary School, Eastbourne
Caitlin Feeney-Miles (9) 108
William Carter (9) 109
James Bezant (10) 109
Chloe Edgar-Connell (9) 109
Leanna Rebaudo (10) 110

Stroud Green Primary School, London
Luke Russell (11) 110
Kofi Odoom (10) 111
Shyante Bucknor 111
Isaac Asher Bracey (10) 112
Koos Osman (11) 112
Joel Falconer (9) 113
Nesrine Benaouda (10) 113
Afia Headley (10) 114
Léo Bouniol (10) 114
Harry Thurlow (11) 115
Ezra Glasstone (10) 115

Tommy Peter Heintz (9)	116
Senanur Duven (9)	116
Joel Milo Robinson (9)	117
Leon Brocklehurst (10)	117
Reece Thomas (10)	118
Zain Hosein (10)	118
Edwina Stewart	118
Sharde	119
Micah Crook (10)	119
Tony Canli (10)	119
Daniel Nicholson (9)	120
Sebek Sturgeon (9)	120
Adina Grant-Adams (10)	120
Olubunmi Oyinka Wabessy (9)	121
Aljay Shackeil Wilson (11)	121
Leon Dunkley (9)	121
Shahzaib Mhamad	122
Cedric Baksh (10)	122
Salma Chakour (11)	122
Darshan Leslie	123
Yaamin Chowdhury (10)	123
Joshua Agbagidi	123

Walter Halls Primary School, Mapperley
Molly Higgins	124
Georgia Bird	125

Warton Nethersole's CE Primary School, Warton
Amy Rose Perkins (11)	126
Alfie Apps (10)	126
Harry Kilkenny (8)	127
Chloe Kimberley (10)	127
Hazelle Whitehead (11)	128
Nathan Daniel Worrall (10)	128
Charlotte Hopkins (10)	129
Ian Ryan (9)	129
Carys Langham (9)	130
Jake Allman (10)	130
Tom Sear (10)	131
Joshua Jones (10)	131
Rebekah Ann Harrison (10)	132
Owen Langham (9)	132
Edward Baker (10)	132

Alice May Briers (10)	133
Katie Harvey (9)	133
Harry White (10)	133
Louise Rose Greenhill (10)	134
Matthew King (9)	134
Jayden Wood (10)	134
Megan Allman (8)	135
Dannie Price (8)	135
Liam Gardner (9)	135
Jack Mason (10)	136
Michael Keeling (9)	136
Georgina Ann Hartop (7)	136
Jacob Sharratt (10)	137
Olivia Hopkins	137
Robyn Turner (7)	137
Izabella Daulman (7)	138
Dayle Lucy Turner (8)	138
Lauren Chapman (7)	138
Tania Critchley (7)	139
Georgia Ann Allbrighton (8)	139
Morgan Norris (8)	139
Owen Collins (7)	140
Jacob Wilson (7)	140
Robbie Barker (10)	140
Ellie Humphries (7)	141
Harriet Critchley (10)	141
Michael Cotterill (10)	141
Joshua Garfield (10)	142
Cameron Adam (8)	142
Nicole & (9) Lizzy (8)	142
Isabelle Hounsome (10)	143
Eleanor Crowley (10)	143
Jaremi Rubin (12)	143

Westways Primary School, Sheffield
Chloe-Louise Storer (11)	144

Whitwick St John the Baptist CE Primary School, Coalville
Eleanor Marlow (7)	144
Abbie Harmer (8)	145
Ellie Harman (7)	145
Ellie Olivia Oldham (8)	146
Kieran Joshua Nutting (7)	146
Dominic Leake (9)	147

Carleigh Attwal (9) 147
Megan Riley (7) 148
Leah Grace Sibson (7) 148
Alice Wilson (9) 148
Abbie Acton (8) 149
Abigail Munro (8) 149
Libby Keeling (7) 149
Emelia Jade Elton (9) 150
Daniel Ward (8) 150

Ysgol Glan Conwy, Colwyn Bay
Sammy Jarvis-Evans 150
Jonathon Coates (10) 151
Owen Parmley (10) 151
Charlotte Wright (10) 152
Becky Jarvis-Evans 152

The Poems

I Love Animals - Haiku

I love animals
No dirty water for pets
Take care of the world.

Bethany Ball (7)
Alcott Hall Primary School, Solihull

Good And Bad Throughout The World

There were cans on the ground
No one cared to look around.

There was paper in the street
Greeting people at their feet.

There were bags in the ocean
Killing animals in their motion.

There was glass in the park
Which left a very dirty mark.

Although we've talked about everything bad
Now let's look at things that make us glad.

There is always someone to help us out
Throughout the world, with no doubt.

Without these people who help us all
We would take a tremendous fall.

With these people who help us all
You could stand very tall.

All this rubbish goes to a tip
And has a very long kip.

This has taken a very long time
Now I can't think of a rhyme.

Luke Boonham (11)
Barlestone CE Primary School, Barlestone

Poverty Of The World

Rich people with massive homes,
Always talking on their mobile phones.
Dipping in their private pool,
Taking their kids to a private school.

Others have none of this,
No luxuries, no bliss.
Starving for a piece of bread,
Some of them are nearly dead.

Is this really very fair,
Knowing that people do not care?
Don't just sit there and do nothing at all,
All you've got to do is make one little call.
Donate some money to charity today,
Or those people will waste away!

Becky Harvey (10), Daisy Forman, Eve & Megan
Barlestone CE Primary School, Barlestone

Rainforests

Animals are now homeless
They're going into despair
We are killing them
Without a care
So let animals free
Without a fee
Trees are being chopped down
And animals wear a frown
So let a cloud become proud
And let a tower become a flower.

Emma Groves & Miranda Ratcliffe (10)
Barlestone CE Primary School, Barlestone

To Die Or Not To Die?

Ever wondered what a dinosaur looked like?
Were they awake all night?
Is it our fault they're not still here?
I don't blame you for shedding a tear.

Dolphins, monkeys and elephants too
Would you miss a bird's sweet coo?
Bunnies and polar bears, do they deserve to die?
I think that I might start to cry.

Can we stop this? I hear you ask
So I'll set you a little task,
Adopt an animal as a pet
Or you could see them at the vet.
There are lots of animals out there to adopt,
So why don't we all just say stop!

Katie Poole & Ashleigh Statham (10)
Barlestone CE Primary School, Barlestone

Extinction

We lose more and more animals every year,
Oh look at these poor animals, dear
We lose tigers and baby crocodiles and polar bears
Also we lose unfortunate baby bears that liked their life,
But they didn't get to finish it because they died.
So please help me save these poor and unfortunate animals
So let's get a move on.

Courtney Marie Jones (10)
Barlestone CE Primary School, Barlestone

Around The World

The world is burning up, we're all feeling sad
And if you could do something, we'd be very glad.

Some people are white, some people are black,
There's no difference and that's a fact.

Planes, buses, cars and boats
The people who do this, hang up your coats.

We're all happy, jolly and good
But across the world they're in the mud.

Rubbish, bottles, paper and sweets,
The birds are dying, let them tweet.

Dolphins, seals, birds and bears
Lots of people don't really care.

Thomas Cooper & Ashley Cooper (11)
Barlestone CE Primary School, Barlestone

Say No To Cars

Think of all those animals dying
It is all because nobody is trying
We can make a difference
By not using cars and biking.

Billy Mugglestone (10) & Macorley
Barlestone CE Primary School, Barlestone

Just Think!

I went to see a show in town
I saw lots of people lying down
My mum said they were homeless and
Had no home town.
It was dirty with rubbish around them
With bins not even full.
Germs and flies are not good
So put your rubbish in the bin like you should.
It smells of smoke
That makes me choke.
So take a walk and get in shape.
When I recycle with my mum I feel really good
About what I've just done.
Glasses and jars, cans and paper
Do your bit, because it will help later.

Cally Smith (8)
Castlecombe Primary School, Mottingham

Save The World

S witch your mind to caring
A bout the future of the planet
V ans and lorries are polluting
E veryone wants to be happy not sad

T he planet is everyone's not just yours.
H elp turn taps off when you are not using them
E very drop counts.

W e are grateful for the world
O ur world is special to us
R ise and shine it is daytime
L ord, thank You for the world
D o it today don't wait for tomorrow.

Emma Coyne
Castlecombe Primary School, Mottingham

Save The World

S end all the rubbish to the bin, *no, no, no*
A nd it will get sent to holes in the ground
V enus is dirty as well as Earth
E verybody does this, it shouldn't be done.

T rees get cut down to make paper and furniture
H elp the world, you really need to just try your best
E nd the journey of holes in the ground.

W onder why the world is not in our minds now
O ur minds are on a planet that makes us feel sad
R ed roses are dying from all the rubbish
L ots of pollution all around
D on't use cars, use a bike, it would be even better to take a *hike!*

Anya Wood (8)
Castlecombe Primary School, Mottingham

Save Our World

S tart recycling, do it now
A lways try to do your best for the planet
V arious creatures are dying
E verybody should ride a bike instead of a car.

O ur planet is shrinking, *help!*
U nder the sea there is lots of rubbish
R ecycling is good for our planet

P lease help our planet!
L eave your car at home, walk instead
A lways put your rubbish in the bin
N ature is dying
E arth is in danger
T he world needs you.

Gracie Davies-Whitehair
Castlecombe Primary School, Mottingham

Save The World

S ave our animals from extinction
A nd protect their natural habitats
V ast areas of natural rainforests are being needlessly cut down
E ncourage our plants to grow healthy and strong.

T he sea levels are rising because of the change in our climate
H elp the environment by doing something today
E arth needs everyone to play their part and protect it.

W alking to school doesn't harm our ozone layer with fumes.
O ur world needs to unite and stamp out war.
R ivers must be kept clean from rubbish and pollution
L itter must not be dropped for it could spread disease
D on't forget to recycle your rubbish because it makes
  our planet a greener place to live in.

Olivia Smithson
Castlecombe Primary School, Mottingham

Save The World

S witch from petrol
A nd use an electric car
V ehicles are very smelly
E veryone could use their wellies!

T ry not to dump litter on the ground or grass,
H elp animals that eat plastic bags
E very creature is dying from it.

W e can stop what is happening
O ld and young still recycle and use
R ubbish goes in the dump
L andfills are getting worse
D o it today and tomorrow.

Samantha-Jaine Ellis
Castlecombe Primary School, Mottingham

Save The World

S witch your mind to caring
A bout the future of this planet
V ote for a clean world
E verybody needs to help because we all are polluting.

T he world needs help from all of us
H elp to save our planet
E arth is in big danger.

W orld needs us
O ur world needs help from all of us
R ecycle all of your rubbish please
L itter should be not around
D on't just do it today, do it now!

Jessie Megan Elliott
Castlecombe Primary School, Mottingham

Save The World

S witch your mind to caring
A bout the future of this planet
V ans and pollution should stop
E xtinction to our animals.

T rees keep on getting chopped down for paper
H elp us to save our world
E nd the diseases.

W hy is there a war?
O xfam helps the world
R ubbish keeps on being dumped on the floor
L itter should be thrown in the bin
D rive your car less and less.

Shannon Hyde (9)
Castlecombe Primary School, Mottingham

Save The World

S tart the recycling right now
A dump might be overflowing
V alleys get bins so put the rubbish in there
E xtra people should take part.

T omorrow may be the end of Planet Earth
H omes of animals probably will get destroyed
E arth will be a dump.

W e should stop now
O ur planet is precious
R eally deep holes get filled every day
L ife's like animals on beaches, it might die
D on't pollute.

Leah Musto (9)
Castlecombe Primary School, Mottingham

Save The World

S top dumping your litter, start recycling
A nimals are our friends, leave their rainforests alone
V ote for a cleaner world
E verybody needs to help because we all make pollution

T errified children, how would you feel?
H elp save our planet
E arth is in big danger.

W alk to school, don't be a litterbug, every little bit helps
O nly you can make a difference
R evolting pollution, nobody wants to breathe that in
L eave the other people's lives alone
D on't give up, help to make the world a better place.

Chelsea Thomas
Castlecombe Primary School, Mottingham

Save The World

S ave our planet
A nd always recycle, it is
V ery important and
E veryone should help.

T hings can be reused, and they don't
H ave to be thrown away
E veryone listen and I will tell you how.

W hen you have a drink
O r have something to eat
R emember to
L ook at the back to see if it can be recycled
D o your bit and save the planet.

Alfie Tilley (8)
Castlecombe Primary School, Mottingham

Save The World

S top the war, people are getting hurt
A nimals dying, save our habitat
V ans are helping cause pollution
E ducate your family

T oday not tomorrow
H elp save the world
E verybody start now

W orldwide problem
O h my God, I can't believe it, everybody's joining in
R ight now
L itter being dropped is affecting the wildlife
D o it now, save our world.

Emily Cox (9)
Castlecombe Primary School, Mottingham

Save The World

S witch lights off when not needed
A lways recycle
V ery important
E veryone is dying in the war

T urtles are dying because you are throwing rubbish
H ear the children screaming
E veryone wears poppies

W hy is war happening?
O ctopi are dying in the sea
R ubbish in the bin
L ights are on when not needed
D ays are dying.

Nathan Conroy (8)
Castlecombe Primary School, Mottingham

Save The World

S ave us all from pollution
A nd stop using the car to get to school
V ery many things are dying
E arth is the best place

T he world will be happy with you
H elp save the environment
E nvironments are precious

W e must stop pollution now!
O ur world would be better
R euse again and again
L et's do things to help
D o it, your world is depending on you.

James Dilley (8)
Castlecombe Primary School, Mottingham

Save The World

S ave the world
A nd the environment
V anish the litter
E arth is our planet

T he world is the best
H ope we have a better life
E arth is our planet

W orld is the best
O ur world can be saved
R ecycling is our hope
L itter is a bad thing
D on't destroy our planet.

Pedro Spinola (7)
Castlecombe Primary School, Mottingham

Save The World

S ave our world
A bout the future of this planet
V ery much pollution spreading
E verybody dumping litter

T ry and help this world
H ave a go at recycling today
E veryone use a bus

W hen you drop litter, think about it
O n your way to the car, think whether you live near a bus stop
R eady, steady, go!
L ook for stuff to recycle
D o it today, don't do it tomorrow.

Jamie Chipping (8)
Castlecombe Primary School, Mottingham

Save The World

S ave our world please
A nimals are dying
V ans and lorries are polluting
E veryone wants to be happy

T rees help keep animals alive
H elp us and it will help you
E ducate everyone please

W hy do we have war?
O ctopi are dying
R emember people that died in the war
L et us be happy
D angerous mines injuring people.

Alfie Mackinnon
Castlecombe Primary School, Mottingham

Save The World

S oldiers are dying
H ow sad!
O ur trees are chopped down, so our animals are homeless
W hy?

Y ou can help can't you?
O ur rubbish can go in the recycling bin
U nderstand what life is like for other people.

C are for animals
A sk questions about how to keep healthy
R escue people so they are saved
E xcuses are not enough!

Rachel Nash (8)
Castlecombe Primary School, Mottingham

Recycling

R ecycling is important
E verybody should do it
'C ause it saves the planet
Y ou should do it too
C an you convince your friends to join with us
L itter should not be anywhere but the recycling bins
I 'm recycling all my rubbish
N ortons do it
G ive it a go too!

Millie Norton
Castlecombe Primary School, Mottingham

Eco-Code

Dustbin says:

I really need to diet!
Look at the size of me.
I'm full to bursting with
Really good food. Why
Do they keep feeding
Me?

        Mr Recycling, that's my name
        Reducing and reusing, that's my game
        There's a fat old dustbin,
        He's a pain!
        They're giving him what
        Should be my gain.

                Why don't
                They feed
                Me
                Instead?

Class 6G (10-11)
Chennestone Primary School, Sunbury

Eco-Code

If we pollute, we'll ruin our world,
So start making changes.

Walk to school, don't be cool,
In a car you won't get far.

There's rubbish here, there's rubbish there,
There's rubbish everywhere.
Pick it up, it's not fair
We have bins everywhere
So put in there.

There's animals here, there's animals there
Show them lots of love and care.

Tree, trees, help us breathe,
Don't cut them down, they give us breeze.
Help the planets, help the trees,
Pull away those nasty weeds.
Plant pretty flowers,
To twinkle in the rain showers.

Close your windows, shut your doors,
Keep the heat indoors.
Lights, lights everywhere,
Turn off if you care.
Without water, how will plants grow,
And where will the fish go?

Class 3W (7-8)
Chennestone Primary School, Sunbury

Eco-Code

We are the green code rappers,
And we have something to say,
We reduce, reuse, recycle,
Every single day.

We reduce what we reuse,
We reuse what we recycle,
Put it all together,
And we have our eco-cycle.

We want the green,
Not the red,
Yeah you heard us,
That's what we said.

If we let our Earth ruin,
It will be a shame,
Composting, using scrap paper,
Is our long-term game.

Keep Earth clean and cool,
Else you won't have it all,
Look at this pollution,
We have a simple solution.
We are cool, we are clean,
We're the greenest school you've ever seen!

Class 6B (10-11)
Chennestone Primary School, Sunbury

Eco-Code

Litter, litter everywhere,
Doesn't anybody care?
The bin is over there!

Please do not leave taps running,
This kind of trick is not stunning,
Instead it's cruel and cunning.

Come on let's recycle things,
Instead of putting things in bins.

Sharing a bath is very fun,
Come on we will soon be done.

Please do not take your car,
If your house is not far!

Chennestone can do it,
So can you!
Come on, there isn't much to do!

Class 4F (8-9)
Chennestone Primary School, Sunbury

Eco-Rap

Don't waste paper when working in school,
Being a paper waster is really not cool,
If you listen to this rap, then you'll turn off the tap,
Don't leave the water to run, that's really not fun!

If you're bright, you will turn off the lights,
Save energy and then we'll be alright,
Put your fruit in a compost bin,
If you don't, that's really a sin!

Grow your own food, that's really useful,
It tastes delicious and keeps us full,
Food makes pollution,
Our allotment is the best solution!

If you do all this, that would be cool,
Because we could be an *eco-school!*

Class 3A (7-8)
Chennestone Primary School, Sunbury

How Could You?

How could you let this happen to me,
Sitting out there in the deep cold sea!

Please help me. My ice could collapse,
Then my home might not be on the maps!

Everyone can save our planet
Together, we can completely ban it!
Your CO_2 is getting rid of my ice,
You could be generous or even nice!
Please help me standing over here
I would prefer to be nowhere near!
Oh please help me and my friend,
Or this thing will never end!

George Welton (11)
Congerstone Primary School, Congerstone

Why?

Why is this happening?
Why should our world suffer?
Why are we doing this, destroying our world?

Why is this happening?
If you were a cute, fluffy, loving polar bear
If you were a nice, big, gentle elephant
If you were a bold, hunting lion
How would you feel?

Why is this happening?
If you were a polar bear, what would happen to you?
If you were a polar bear, would you survive?
If you were a polar bear, how long would you last?
I know why this is happening,
It's us, we are the problem!

There are many solutions like:
Save energy!
Recycle!
Reduce your carbon footprint!
Only use what you need!

Help save the environment,
In any way you can!

Do you want to see the world
As a dark and lonely place?
Do your bit
Our world will not survive
Unless you help!

Emma Kelwin (10)
Congerstone Primary School, Congerstone

Save The World!

If you want to be the bee's knees
Then keep all our trees,
If metal is recycled you could,
Buy a new bicycle.

Litter is bad,
If you drop litter you must be mad.
That's why there's bins!

Walk to school,
Don't hop in the car,
Or bike to school,
Don't jump in the car!

Save our animals
Please don't be horrible,
Don't send them to the circus,
Let them be free!

Animals are in trees, remember!
So when you cut down trees,
The animals' homes are gone.

Save our water, don't waste it away,
Eat our food, don't throw it away.

Don't use up all our energy.
Turn your heating down,
And turn your lights off!

Ellie Jane Lawrence (11)
Congerstone Primary School, Congerstone

What Are We Doing?

What are we doing to our world?
We are destroying the place where we live.
Only we can put it right,
Forests are now cities full of bright light.

Polar bears will become extinct,
Maybe only another 100 years.
Would you want to see them die?
I don't think it's fair, do you?

Our world was peaceful,
We can change everything if we try.
Can't you hear the animals while they cry?

The world is wonderful,
Keep it that way,
Children, us, we still want forests to play,
You are the destroyers,
Just stop!

Leaves once fell,
We played in them,
Animals ran,
Now they are scared, some dead,
Just stop and think.

What are we doing to our world?
Don't make it an unhappy place!

Jasmine Towersey (9)
Congerstone Primary School, Congerstone

What's The World Coming To?

What is the world coming to?
Where are the forests going?
Where are the countrysides going?
Are they running away or are they going to be chopped down by Man
And made into shops and houses?

Where are the animals going?
Are the big whales crying and the polar bears dying
And the elephants running away
Because Man is trying to poach them?

What is the world coming to?
Are we going to destroy our planet and create a hole
In the ozone layer?

Money isn't everything you know,
There is one thing money can't buy,
That is love and if you follow your heart,
You will find love and happiness!

There is one big question and that is, is the world going to die?

Think!

Would you like it if you were the last one of your species?
Would you like it if you had no one to love you?

*Save the world by helping
Instead of destroying it!*

Emily-Jayne Marston (9)
Congerstone Primary School, Congerstone

I Am A Polar Bear! I Am Big And Proud!

Will this be the end?
Will it be the end of the world!
Will it?

Use your heart
It is the only way!
There is no other.

I am a polar bear!
I am big and proud!
I am!

We blend in but not for long!
We live in a kingdom of glory
But not for long!

We help Man
Now you help us!
Help by turning your dishwasher down
To 30° and your heater.
Walk not drive!
Please help me!
Help my species
We are dying
We are!

I am going under with the *rest!*

Thomas Paice (10)
Congerstone Primary School, Congerstone

Is It Our Fault?

Is it our fault?
Because ice caps are shrinking,
Polar bears have lost their homes.
Should we start thinking?

Is it our fault?
Because rainforests are being cut down,
Animals are becoming extinct.
Please do not frown.

Is it our fault?
Because tigers are dying out,
Animals get hunted down.
Please do not shout.

Is it our fault?
Can we save the planet?
Can we do something now?
We should just *ban* it!

Look at this poem,
Please do think,
This *is* our fault!
Please, please think.
Polar bears can't stay for long.

Liberty Jackson (10)
Congerstone Primary School, Congerstone

Save The Bear

What are we doing to our only Earth?
Will the fields still be green or will they be covered in tarmac?

Just give the Earth a chance
Right this minute the Earth is dying.
What about the polar bear guarding his crystal cave?
Thinking to himself, my kingdom awaits.
The big polar bear clinging onto a single ice cap.
Poor thing.

Stop cutting down my habitat, it's where I live.
C'mon what have we ever done to you?
I'll be on my own.
There's only a few of us out here.
Do you want to see the polar bear fade away, disappearing into
                                             the dark?
Because that's what you're doing at the moment.
Polar bears live in a kingdom of glory, but not for long!
The polar bears are strong and they're fighters!

Think before you throw rubbish to the ground,
Think before you throw rubbish in the ocean.
Think!

Rheo Parnell (9)
Congerstone Primary School, Congerstone

What Are We Worth?

Factories, pollution and fumes
They are ruining the Earth
And so are we.
What is the Earth worth?

The ice caps are shrinking
And polar bears are scared,
Maybe we should start thinking
And be prepared.

We can save this place
If we really try our best
And save every race
We can be better than the rest.

Do you want your children to see
All the lovely things on Earth
Like the polar bear running free?
What is the Earth worth?

Do you want to
See these wonderful creatures in 100 years?
Think, they are in your hands.

Victoria Riley (10)
Congerstone Primary School, Congerstone

Albatross And Others

I fly over the ozone
Ice melting everywhere,
I see my friends all drowning,
Sinking in despair.

I fear it is all my fault
Not diving in triumph,
But when I go next morning,
There's a carcass so lifeless.

I feel so sad,
For the Arctic ice,
So *please* come on.

The time is running out too fast,
So when you're ready,
Give a shout.

The last polar bears are struggling,
The babies are getting cold
So now they're huddling
Around their mum,
Will their life be good or glum?

Clarice May Benney (9)
Congerstone Primary School, Congerstone

Hey, I'm A Polar Bear

Hey, I'm a polar bear
And I need a lot of care
Please don't let pollution kill me
I will sink to the bottom of the sea
Please . . .
Don't kill me!

There's nowhere to stroll now, in the North Pole
I'm about to enter a big black hole
I'm getting warmer,
My time is getting shorter
Please . . .
Don't kill me!

Soon my home won't be on the map
I feel like I'm under attack
Please fix the ozone layer quickly
Stop the planet being so sickly!

Hey, I'm a polar bear
Please . . .
Don't kill me!

Kai Tannicliffe (9)
Congerstone Primary School, Congerstone

Stop It!

Why are you cutting trees?
Please stop, please!

Hey stop cutting them down,
Quick plant some *now!*
Definitely away from town!

Why are you cutting down trees?
Please stop, please.

Yes, the Earth is in danger,
Everyone become an eco-ranger.

Why are you cutting down trees?
Please stop! Please!

Help save the Earth
Because sometimes it's worth it to be in the universe!

Please stop animals becoming extinct,
Please think, just think!

I'm a polar bear, help me, I might cry,
If you don't help me, *I will die!*

Jack Collin (10)
Congerstone Primary School, Congerstone

Why Is This Happening?

Why are ice caps melting?
Polar bears dying,
Hanging onto ice for their lives,
Struggling to find food.

> Why can't we save animals like these?
> Polar bears, penguins, whales and fish
> Are all struggling,
> Pollution is bubbling.

Why are we not changing?
Stop throwing your rubbish wherever you like,
Don't drive the car,
Go on your bike!

> Why is this happening?
> Polar bears' homes are shrinking
> Ice caps melting
> What were we thinking?

Start being green now!

Leah Rutley (10)
Congerstone Primary School, Congerstone

Bear Factor

We shouldn't be doing this.
Don't let them die.
Don't let the icebergs slowly go.
Come on, let's bring back all the snow.
So! Turn off the lights. Turn off the TV. Turn off the taps,
Singing 1, 2, 3.
We are doing wrong.
We should help the bears
Turn the washers to 30 and it still gets out the dirty.
People shouldn't be doing this. Don't make them die.
Come on and bring back all the snow.
Hey guys, come on, this is a big issue, so, no, no, no, no.
We're doing wrong.
So we need to stop.
Come on everybody, just give it a shot.
So! turn off the lights and the TV. Turn off the taps singing 1, 2, 3.
Hey, hey, hey!
I wanna save energy.

Sam Bridle (9), Finn Campton & Owen Blythe (10)
Congerstone Primary School, Congerstone

Polar Bears!

How do you stop the ice caps melting?
How do we stop the polar bears dying?
Let's start trying and stop people crying.
Our CO_2 is nothing, yet I know it's killing animals
And us too.
I hope you care because it's not fair
Those poor things might not live out there in a pair.
Those poor fluffy bears are white and cute.
I hope we can stop it or they will die!
    Just think!

Harriet Moss (11)
Congerstone Primary School, Congerstone

Where Are You?

Where are you?
Are you hidden in winds that blow
Or are you made out of heaps of snow?

Save the world or it will break.
You don't want that for goodness sake!

Where are you?
Are you with a polar bear feeling sad
Or are you at school being bad?

Save the world and we'll feel proud
If you don't we'll be like a cloud.

Where are you?
Are you crawling around with the rats
Or are you in caves with the bats?

Will you find me, or will I be stuck?
All I need is patience and a little luck.

Daisy Handford (10)
Congerstone Primary School, Congerstone

Save Me!

I am a polar bear!
I love my ice palace, now look at it!
Can you give me some care?
Our kingdom is heaven, so don't destroy it
Be fair!
You wouldn't like to live there!
Please don't tear me away from my habitat
Try and spare me
Just give me a chance!
Save the polar bears!
Help!

Ryan Gordon (9)
Congerstone Primary School, Congerstone

Why Is It Possible?

Why is it possible for this to happen?
Hopefully it won't.
It's making me so sad.
I don't think I can stop it,
It's making me mad!
Will you stop wasting energy?
Do it for me.
If you don't just try it, you will never see.
If you won't stop pollution, then I will!
Come on, if you don't just try it you will never see.
Why is it possible for the world to change?
It used to be brilliant, it will never be the same
If you don't just try it you'll never have fame.
Why is it possible?

Niamh Harriman (10)
Congerstone Primary School, Congerstone

Hey There Polar Bear!

Hey there polar bear,
What are you doing over there,
Clinging onto a piece of ice,
Hanging on for your dear life?

Global warming my dear friend,
And now I'm about to meet my end.
You could have saved me.
You're not very caring,
Take my home and yours, now start comparing!
All us polar bears are not at ease,
We'd really like some conservation please.
So please, please, please help spread the word,
And maybe you could help save the world.

Will Abell (10)
Congerstone Primary School, Congerstone

Who Am I?

Who am I?
Global warming is making it too hot for our species.
Who am I?
Our lives are changing and we need your help
Who am I?
I'm brave, I'm strong.
Who am I?
I'm super, I can be a terror!
Who am I?
I am lots of things. I'm brave, sleek, handsome and a terror,
A diver, a swimmer.
When I was a youngster I was cute, fluffy and very lovable . . .
But now, I want to be me,
A polar bear, please save me!

Kitty Handford (9)
Congerstone Primary School, Congerstone

The Polar Bear!

The polar bear was on the ice
Acting all sweet and nice.
The fish below the giant bear,
Could see the white and fluffy hair.
The huge polar bear leapt gracefully in,
Tearing off the fish's fin.
There was red blood all around her jaw,
She was tearing the fish apart, with her claw.
She took the fish back to her cub,
Then she gave the cub a rub.
Then they all went to sleep,
In a big, white, cuddly heap,
The ice came back and they travelled far, far away!

Morgan Lock (9)
Congerstone Primary School, Congerstone

What Will My Future Be?

What will my future be on Earth?
Will there be any elephants left or rhinos?
Will there be any animals left?
When I'm grown up, will I even survive?
Why am I doing this?
Will the whale cry or will my cat die?
Will my grandchildren ever see the magnificent tiger roaring free?
Will they ever see a tree?
Will they be free and see what we can see?
Will their faces be free and happy to think about all of those things
That might not be here in many years?
Can the world survive?
Will there be any fish swimming in the sea,
Or will they have died out?

Catherine Abell (8)
Congerstone Primary School, Congerstone

My Place

My place is a wonderful place
It's mine and I like it.

Do you like it?
But if you do why do you fill it
With rubbish and fuel?

Please don't do it, it's
Cruel, cruel, *cruel!*

My place is a wonderful place
It's mine, please don't break it.

I'm proud and strong but not for long,
I'll be swimming on my own.

Charlotte Vasey (10)
Congerstone Primary School, Congerstone

Where Has It Gone?

Where has it gone?
The golden leaves in autumn
What is there instead? Nothing . . . nothing . . .
Where are the foxes in their burrows?
What is there instead, a deer park?
No! There is an industrial estate
Can you see so many animals have been harmed by this monstrosity!
When will I ever hear the wolves' howl of happiness?
This is our only chance to change, so make a difference!

I am a lonely polar bear, where is my family?
There is no one left . . .

Harry Talbot (10)
Congerstone Primary School, Congerstone

Save Me!

There's polar bears out there clinging to ice
Like a monkey holding a banana.

Hey there polar bear, what you doing there?
You better hang on there.

There are lots of ice caps melting every day
All this is caused by you!

To stop all this you need to:
Save energy, cycle
Recycle, don't use cars all the time
Stop wasting water
Stop pollution now!

Josh Cumbley (11)
Congerstone Primary School, Congerstone

Please Stop Crying

When I grow up will polar bears die?
Will we stop hearing the wolves' howling cry?
How do we save plants and trees?
Oh come on God, help us please!
The best thing to do is pick up conkers, pine cone seeds
Don't pick the leaves off trees!
Plant them somewhere, where plants are old and dying.

Come on humpback whale, please stop crying!
And when the tree has grown, don't cut it down, leave it alone!

Take some time to think, who's to blame?
Life is not about fortune and fame.

Sophie Wilkins (8)
Congerstone Primary School, Congerstone

Use Your Heart

Use your ears, can you hear the whale cry?
Use your eyes, can you see the world changing?
Use your nose, can you smell the litter?
Use your hand, can you feel the sadness?
I am using my ears, I am using my head,
I am using my eyes and nose, but I still need *help!*

Then use your legs, walk the way you think is right!
Use your arms, just hold on to what you believe is right!
I am using my arms and I am using my legs, but *I still need help!*

Then touch your heart and reach for your soul, you can do it!
Don't hold back! *Save the world!*

Joshua Jones (10)
Congerstone Primary School, Congerstone

Why?

P lease stop pollution, you're destroying my home.
O ur planet needs your help now!
L owering your washing machine temperature could save polar bears
A re you doing the best you can? Think
R ealise what you have done to me!

B e proud about what you believe in!
A re you doing the best you can? Think!
E ffortlessly, you could change my life!
R egroup and save me!
S ave me, you have the power!

Bradley McLean (10)
Congerstone Primary School, Congerstone

How Do We Save Our Planet?

P lease help me stop this!
O nly we can stop this
L et's get together
A ct fast
R eact to this now.

B ears need your help
E fficiency is needed
A ccomplish our target
R earrange what we did
S ave our planet!

Mackenzie Moore (9)
Congerstone Primary School, Congerstone

Save The World!

Save the world! Save it now!
Pandas, tigers, all dying out,
Polar bears won't hang about,
Rainforests collapsing,
I don't know, is it all happening?

Plagues are trying!
People are dying!
So quit the car and walk instead,
Or all the pandas will be dead,
So save the world, save it now!

Joshua Munroe (8)
Congerstone Primary School, Congerstone

Polar Bear

P lease everyone, help the polar bear
O ur planet is getting hotter
L et us do something because there is only 20-25,000 in the wild
A re we going to do nothing and let them become extinct?
R eady everyone, save the planet.

B ears are special things, we don't want them to become extinct
E verybody stop using energy
A ll polar bears could be extinct in 100 years
R eady everyone, be an eco-warrior and save them!

Harry Payne (11)
Congerstone Primary School, Congerstone

Save The Bear

Stop global warming, save the bear
Save its fluffy hair
They may seem gruffy
But I told you they're fluffy
So save the polar bear.

They're lonely
They're struggling
For their kingdom
They will cry, they will yelp
Until we give them our help.

George Holmes (10)
Congerstone Primary School, Congerstone

The Packet

This is the packet that came from the supermarket that lives in the
House where Alec lives
This is the bin that eats the packet that came from the supermarket
That lives in the house where Alec lives
This is the lorry that collects the bin that holds the packet that came
From the supermarket that came to the house where Alec lives
This is the dump that the packet has been thrown in that came from
The lorry that picked up the bin that came from the house where Alec lives
This is soil that came from the packet that rots from the dump that
Came in the lorry that picked up the bin that came from the house where
Alec lives
These are the poisons that fed the plant that came from the soil
That came from the packet that rots in the dump that came in
The lorry that picked up the bin where Alec lives.
This is the *shock* that Alec got from eating the plant that grew in the
Soil that came from the lorry that picked up the bin that held the
Packet that lived in the house where Alec lived.

Alec Deakin (7)
Dragon School, Oxford

Acid Rain

What caused the acid rain to fall?
Does anybody know?
It's us that caused it to
Rain down hard
It's us that caused it to flow
And now it falls on
Grass
Falls on
Plains
Falls on
Flowers
Falls on
Trains
Falls on
Trees
Falls on
Grain
Acid rain
Acid
Rain
Ac
Id
R
A
I
N.

Orlando Riviere (7)
Dragon School, Oxford

Help Me - Haiku

It's very unfair
I'm stuck in the cold and rain
Help me I am sick.

Cian Ellis (7)
Dragon School, Oxford

Stop Pollution

I am such a lonely fish
For all my friends have died.
They couldn't even make a wish,
They drowned in pesticide.

And I'm a lonely polar bear
My friends are far away,
Because there is no ozone layer
We have nowhere to play.

And I'm a lonely little fox,
I have no mum or dad
They ate some poison in a box
And now I am so sad.

And I'm a lonely little bird
There's nothing I can eat
The yummy bugs have disappeared
Because of so much heat.

And I'm a lonely little girl
There'll soon be nothing good
If nasty things pollute this world
We'll all run out of food.

Flora Smiley (8)
Dragon School, Oxford

Recycle

R ecycle, I know that you can
E arly and fast - as quick as the wind
C an't you stop cutting down those trees?
Y oung people sitting in the street
C ut the smoke from the factories
L eaving rubbish on the ground - to
E njoy it - cut it down!

Henry Williams (8)
Dragon School, Oxford

The Air

The air was poisonous
The sea was crashing against angry rocks
And flowed into the street
And simply crashed back into the sea.

But there was a sudden movement
And the sea came roaring back
As a shark swam in fear
It silently simply stopped
It was out of rage.

It did not slither
In the still
Dark
Night
In
The
Black
Sea for
A
Long
Time.

Tiggy Greenfield (8)
Dragon School, Oxford

Pollution

If the air is polluted
Go to tell the Queen
And tell her it is not fair
We really need to be green.

You have to turn off the lights
Computer and consoles to be right
Save energy!

Alexander Bellenie (7)
Dragon School, Oxford

Water

             Water rushes
           As the rain falls
              Thunder threatens
                  As storm clouds call
              Streams swell
          And
           Rivers rush
         Animals
       Hide
     Under the
   Holly bush
The rainbow
    Climbs
      As the
       Sun
         Bursts through
     A golden light
       Comes
      Into
     View.

Gus Cayzer (8)
Dragon School, Oxford

Hurricane

A savage, freaky hurricane,
Spinning and turning.
Making chaos around the world,
Destruction and burning.

Hurricanes out of control,
Mayhem and whirling.
Winds of 200 miles per hour,
That's global warming.

Alec Michaelis (8)
Dragon School, Oxford

Trees

I walked down the street
It looked very neat
There were trees everywhere
And birds in the air.

I walked down the street
It was another day
The trees had gone
And the birds had flown away.

I used to feed the birds
But now they've gone away
Because nature is changing
It's so hard to say!

But it's not fair!

Flora Frankopan (7)
Dragon School, Oxford

Antarctica

Antarctica used to be cool
But now it's like a melting swimming pool.

A pool is a place to share
But what about the polar bear?

Climate change is rather bad
And it seems extremely sad.

The ice is melting faster than ever
And it looks like we're not going to help, never!

We are all being terribly cruel
And we are using more petrol and fuel.

It really is up to us *all!*

Jacob Bright (8) & Rhodri Whiteley (7)
Dragon School, Oxford

Recycling

Recycle, recycle bottles and cans,
Recycle, recycle, everyone can.
Who recycles? I don't know,
It's very distracting, can someone show?
Maybe I should start recycling too?
That's what I think I should do!

I know, I know, I will pick up a can,
And then please do it, every child, woman and man.
I'll recycle, I'll tidy up,
That's amazing, I want to jump!

Please recycle, please join in,
Please don't put it in the bin
But . . . *recycle!*

Amelia Whinney (7)
Dragon School, Oxford

Pollution

Pollution is happening to the Earth
It's acting worse than at its birth
And that's when it is exploded
Countries like here are getting overloaded
With water. The hot countries on the Equator
Don't have very much life-giving water
The seas are getting really dirty
And some are getting pretty murky
People are being very cruel
Using and wasting too much fuel.

Joshua van der Merwe (7)
Dragon School, Oxford

Litter

R ubbish should never be thrown on the floor
U nder the bin lid there is only a shiny bit of tin
B ut nothing can stop those evil pests from throwing litter on the floor
B ut if you pick it up they still chuck it on the floor
I sn't it so irritating for people having to pick up other people's junk?
S o pick it up now
H ate rubbish. Love recycling.

Jamie Volak (8)
Dragon School, Oxford

Pollution

P eople are polluting!
O h the Earth is dying!
L iving fish are being killed
L iving plants are being destroyed
U are taking part in this
T ill this stops you will suffer
I n the future this could get better
O n the Earth people are polluting
N ot enough people are paying attention.

Anthony Monaco
Dragon School, Oxford

Global Warming

Dark days of carbon dioxide
Few tropical trees breathe out oxygen
Sunlight and heat warms up the atmosphere
Destroying our Earth.

Luke Miles
Dragon School, Oxford

Horrid People

People are very horrid
Like Goldilocks who stole porridge
They squirt graffiti on the wall
And go through town and be like fools
My heart goes *beat, beat, beat*
And then I speak.
I don't like horrid people!
Clean up this mess and don't be a pest
And be nice like the rest of us.

Tom Willcox (7)
Dragon School, Oxford

Pollution

P lease everybody, stop pollution
O r we wouldn't have such a lovely world
L ove the world that God gave to us
L ove the flowers, see the rivers
U nder the trees, see the rivers
T rust nature
I nvent safe energy
O pen our minds
N o more pollution.

Annabel Cave (7)
Dragon School, Oxford

Recycle

Recycle, recycle rubbish and rusty cans,
Recycle, recycle, don't chuck rubbish on the floor!
What we need to do is recycle
That sounds like a fantastic idea.

Maya Stern (7)
Dragon School, Oxford

Recycling

I like recycling, it's the best thing
I know it's just so revolting
When it's on the floor
Can you help me get rid of it?
It's so annoying when it's on the floor
I wish you could get rid of it
I hope you help me
Recycle!

Tom Mills (7)
Dragon School, Oxford

Recycle

R ecycle paper and cardboard
E lastic bands and
C ans
Y ou and me need to reuse
C lear plastic bottles are also
L ovely to reuse with new water
E lastic bands you find on the street and you can use them again.

Poppy Webb (7)
Dragon School, Oxford

Recycle

R ecycle for the environment
E verything will be told to the government
C ome on, you don't have to be grumpy
Y ou will have people who are much happier
'C ause if you are green you will be chirpier
L ove the world, it is our only hope.
E nvironment needs to work - it is all up to you.

Alexandra Kosobucki (7)
Dragon School, Oxford

Animals

Why are people ruining animals' homes?
I hate hearing that animals have been made extinct
Tigers, pandas and bears.
Animals are nice to have
It is sad when they are extinct
Do not pollute the world, it is bad for the animals
Please do not.

Jenny Hannah (7)
Dragon School, Oxford

Haikus

Recycle today
Reuse your water bottles
Reduce energy!

Reduce newspapers
Start doing it right now please
Pollution is bad!

Saskia Orr
Dragon School, Oxford

Untitled - Haikus

I am worried that
The people on the street will
Soon suffer for food.

The people on streets
With their dogs lie on the street
People just walk past.

Rose Rooney (7)
Dragon School, Oxford

Homeless In London - Haikus

I am very sad
I am very cold and wet
I feel sorrowful.

I am unhappy
I can see dew on the ground
I am freezing too.

Charlotte Hope (7)
Dragon School, Oxford

Untitled - Haikus

Frustrated people
Begging on the London streets,
Soulless, dejected.

Completely damaged
In the cold winter it is
Snowing, I hate them.

Jack Stacey (7)
Dragon School, Oxford

Litter

L itter is bad, don't do it
I think littering is really bad
T o be a good person, don't pollute
T o recycle put rubbish in the bin
E at everything you are given
R ecycle - do it!

Ollie Brown (7)
Dragon School, Oxford

Litter

L oads of people drop litter everywhere and I don't like it
I never drop litter because it's polluting our world
T owns sometimes have litter
T ons of fields have pollution
E arth has been polluted by litter
R ubbish - you should pick up litter.

India Deakin (7)
Dragon School, Oxford

Stop!

A nimals are very nice to have in the world
N obody should kill them
I really want people to stop
M etal rusty things everywhere too!
A nd it makes me want to cry!
L itter and extinct animals really worry me.

Catherine Churchill (8)
Dragon School, Oxford

Litter

L itter is bad
I have to stop
T ry to recycle
T ry to put rubbish in the recycling bin
E at everything you are served so it is not a waste
R ecycling is very good.

Rachel Oldershaw (7)
Dragon School, Oxford

Meltdown

The snowcapped mountains are loaded with ice
We must help in the fight
We are ruining the world and landscape
We destroy animals' homes
Please stop and think what you are doing
And help us save the planet.

Tom van Oss (8)
Dragon School, Oxford

Litter

L eaving litter
I s bad
T ry to recycle
T ry not to leave litter on the ground
E veryone can
R ecycle, please recycle, I'll do it!

Lucy Hope (7)
Dragon School, Oxford

Don't Drop Litter

Recycle, recycle bottles and cans
Recycle; everybody can.
Save electricity, don't use cars
Don't drop litter on the floor
Put it in the bin and use bicycles instead.

Charlie Girelli-Kent (7)
Dragon School, Oxford

Untitled - Haiku

I'm invisible
I am frightened in the cold
Help me I am sick.

Katia Theologis (7)
Dragon School, Oxford

A Homeless Man - Haiku

'Can you help me please?'
'Are you cold in the night-time?
That is *very sad!*'

Maddie Campion (7)
Dragon School, Oxford

Rainy Day - Haiku

I am done for now
And nobody respects me
Cold and wet and damp.

Charlie McCammon (8)
Dragon School, Oxford

Living On The Streets - Haiku

I feel unhappy
I feel very terrible
On a dark cold night.

Katarina Frankopan (7)
Dragon School, Oxford

On The Streets - Haiku

I am worried that
People on the streets will soon
Suffer from hunger.

Katherine Cochrane (7)
Dragon School, Oxford

Storm - Haiku

It is stormy now
He is invisible now
Who will help this man?

Sebastian Ingham (7)
Dragon School, Oxford

Untitled - Haiku

I am so sick, I'm
Stuck on a damp, windy night
I need lots of help.

Harriet Harries-Jones (7)
Dragon School, Oxford

Untitled - Haiku

I am not rubbish
Please help me, I'm very sick
I just have my dog.

Stella Cohen (7)
Dragon School, Oxford

Haiku

Pollution is bad
People are making it hot
Please stop, stop and stop.

Emma Wheatland (7)
Dragon School, Oxford

Save!

Save all the trees
And the cocoa beans!
If we run out of flowers,
We'll run out of honey and bees!

If the pollution goes too far,
We'll all have to go to Mars!
If we run out of vines,
We won't have any wines!

If you don't start looking after
Our planet,
You won't have any air . . .

To breathe!

Marisa Orton (9)
Elton CE Primary School, Elton

This Is How My Puppy Sees Nature

I have furry feet that squelch on the grass.
Go out the back, I don't need a pass.
Out I go but not too slow
I walk by a leaf and see a caterpillar grow.
I think of the future to see whether it's pretty
I try not to go out in the great big city.
I walk a bit further and what do I see?
But a frog jumping very happily.
He tried to tell me what happened to his water
It was polluted except a little quarter
So you could help a bit more
By not breaking the eco-law.

Holly Nicholls (7)
Llancarfan Primary School, Llancarfan

Life Forever

Spiders, ladybirds, woodlice and bees,
Do not squash them, let them be free.
Also our rainforests need the trees to stay pretty green.
Put your litter in the bin every day,
And do not drop it so it can fly away.
Please look after the beautiful flowers
And give them extra love so they can blossom with powers,
Like the golden sun.

Nicole Lawson (8)
Llancarfan Primary School, Llancarfan

Bringing Earth To Life

Reduce, reuse, recycle,
It's a great way of making a difference,
Do it today!

Animals endangered,
Plants are dying too,
Let's make a difference,
What can you do?

Trees provide oxygen,
So that we breathe,
If we cut them down,
Our lives may not succeed.

Out there somewhere,
War is going on
It's not a great thing for helping someone.

Respect each other,
And try to get along,
That way, we will be happy,
And we will be strong.

Melting ice caps is a big issue,
Using your car less is helpful too.

Litter on the pavement,
Litter on the floor,
Put it in the bin, then there won't be anymore.

So listen to this message
Of what is going on
Can you help and be someone?

Laura Billingham (10)
Lutley Primary School, Halesowen

The World At Its Worst

Do you feel the guilt?
In our world today,
Years of constant worry,
Do you think it's OK?

The big three Rs,
That's what we need to do,
Reduce, reuse, recycle,
It'll work for you.

Can you hear the world
Crying out for help?
Listen to the falling trees
Just listen, hear them yelp.

Fighting, suffering, dying,
What a great, great shame,
Soldiers risking their lives for us,
And we don't do the same.

What about Red Nose Day?
Do you know what it's for?
It helps unfortunate lives,
For children who are sick or poor.

So there it is in one,
The world at its worst today,
Let's go and save our planet,
Help make a change today.

Heather Pope (10)
Lutley Primary School, Halesowen

Save The World

Reduce, reuse, recycle,
That's what we must do.
Reduce, reuse, recycle,
All work together me and you.

Stop all the wars
Make the world a better place,
Stop all the wars,
Or it will be the end of the human race.

Save the rainforests,
Animals dying in the cold,
Save the rainforests,
Let's break the mould.

Buy Fairtrade,
It will be fair,
Buy Fairtrade,
Flip a coin if you dare.

Children in need,
Let's all think,
Children in need,
We can save them in a blink.

So let's save the world today,
Hip hip hooray!

Amber Barnsley (11)
Lutley Primary School, Halesowen

Make The World A Better Place

To make the world a better place,
Try to protect the human race,
Stop the wars straightaway,
Bring our troops home today,
To put a big smile on our face.

Children in Need, leave it to us,
We do not want to make a fuss,
Please show some consideration,
By making a kind donation,
Because children depend on us.

Recycling do it today,
There are a few rules to obey,
Put waste in the green bin,
Paper, plastic and tin,
Think about what you throw away.

Rainforests are being destroyed,
Indigenous people annoyed,
More endangered creatures,
Disappearing features,
The world's landscape will have a void.

Katie Wrighton (10)
Lutley Primary School, Halesowen

Help Save The World!

Reduce, reuse, recycle, that's what we need to do,
We must think about the planet, let's see what it does for you.
It provides us with oxygen, so that we can breathe,
Animals and plants we should be proud of what we can achieve,
Litter on the street, please just pick it up,
It may not be yours, but don't let it erupt.

War is going on, it's such a terrible thing,
This is why we should keep the peace, just let it out and sing,
Do you love the rainforest? I'm sure I do,
But it's being chopped down, we need to think this through,
Can you help the orang-utan who doesn't have long to live?
Yes just donate a tree, that's all you have to give.

Over in Africa, children have no home,
Children in Need support this as results are shown,
Please help us make the world a better place,
Otherwise this will be the end of the human race,
We're not really asking for much,
Just with a magic touch,
All this madness will go away,
So help right now, start today.

Sophie Hughes (11)
Lutley Primary School, Halesowen

Stop

We need to respect,
You just have to accept,
It's all about debating,
Yet still carry on hating.

We need to keep building,
But there is not enough helping.
We need to stop the war,
Let's show this thing the door.

We need to make some schools,
And have a few more rules.
So let's save a few more plants,
And help the leaf cutting ants.

We're destroying their habitat,
There is a lot of harm to that.
They will start to die out,
You'll never see a crocodile snout.

Help please!

George Wakeman (11)
Lutley Primary School, Halesowen

Help Now!

We need to communicate,
And settle it on a debate,
Because we have to respect the law,
As people are dying in the war.

We need to give to Children in Need,
And you would be doing a good deed,
If you just go and give,
Children in need have more chance to live.

Yelp, yelp, yelp,
The children in Africa need your help,
You are getting rid of the trees,
And you are destroying habitats of the bees.

People in war have made a sacrifice,
So they would want the world to be nice,
You could at least make the world a better place
Then you would give people who went to war a smile on their face.

Michael Eaton (10)
Lutley Primary School, Halesowen

Making A Better Place!

Adults go out not knowing if they will come back,
So please cut them a bit of slack,
Red Nose Day and Mufty too,
People out there just don't have a clue.

Try to save paper
Along with the endangered tapir,
Some could suffer with disease,
So help the children please, please,
Follow the rules and life will be
A much better place for you and me.

Lydia Hanson (10)
Lutley Primary School, Halesowen

Around The World!

Around the world it's getting too bad,
The rainforest matter is making me mad.
Some animals are soon going to be crying,
For some help because they might be dying.

Wars are starting every year,
That is what people need to hear,
People are dying every day,
For other people to get their own way.

Children in Need are raising money,
To make people's world nice and sunny.
Children need good education,
As well as good medication.

So this is why we need to help,
And try and stop people having to yelp.
The world is an important place,
So this is a very strong case.

Megan Abbie Morris (10)
Lutley Primary School, Halesowen

Heal The World

Heal the world, don't cut down the trees,
Animals will become extinct,
Insects and the variety of leaves,
Encourage people to buy Fairtrade,
Where you know that products are fairly made,
Reduce, reuse, recycle, that's all we have to do,
Cans, tins and paper too, being made into something new.
We are losing our population,
And ruining God's creation,
So please heal the world!

Samantha Rostron (10)
Lutley Primary School, Halesowen

Heart, Effort, Love, Perseverance

Why is the world in war?
I hope this is no more.

Remake, reduce, recycle
Just use the three Rs
Forget your cars.

Please use Fairtrade
Things are fairly made.

Make the world a better place
A thing that we can face.

Be generous and give
Let the others live.

Don't judge them on the colour of their skin
No you shouldn't wag your chin

So thank you for listening.

Roshni McCarthy (10)
Lutley Primary School, Halesowen

Save Our Planet

Recycle paper, plastic and cans
Don't put them in rubbish vans
Put your rubbish in recycling bins
Don't forget to put in your metal tins
Save electricity, don't spill oil
Because then rainforests won't spoil
Don't make the world seem like it's bad
Because animals and us will be sad
Pudsey bear and all his friends
Help this world that never ends!

Olivia Symes (10)
Lutley Primary School, Halesowen

Try To Save The World!

Why don't you help the world today?
By standing up to have your say.
Trade, war and poverty,
So make other people see,
That this today is not dismay.

Use less paper, recycle it,
Why don't you walk instead of sit?
Don't let animals die,
Change now, give it a try,
Help the world by a tiny bit.

Help more people get clean water,
Let them have more than a quarter,
Pudsey and Red Nose Day,
This is not just fun play,
This is helping the world, sorta.

Ellie Bryan (11)
Lutley Primary School, Halesowen

Help Our Planet!

Help us to save the Earth,
Until death, from your birth
If you have already helped Children in Need
Stop extinction of trees, plant a seed.
Ice caps are melting,
Reduce, reuse, recycle, are you helping?
In the rainforest, trees are cut down,
Too many lights are on in the town.
Wars are going on today,
Listen to each other, respect and pray,
Become sustainable, grow vegetables and fruit,
Everyone can make a difference if they follow suit.

Agnes Ranford (10)
Lutley Primary School, Halesowen

Bring Us Peace . . .

Santa
Bring us peace
Make those children happy
Who do not have family there
With them

Children
Do not worry
There is no need to cry
People in the world will help you
Achieve

Peace
Will be coming
They will be back soon
Just hold on a little more to
Your heart.

Sophie Griffiths (10)
Lutley Primary School, Halesowen

Save The Earth!

Try to save all of the paper,
Along with all of the tapirs,
Just come on and save the Earth!

Soon enough you'll kill all of the cheetahs
And all of the anteaters
Now that wouldn't be nice at all.

So don't kill any trees,
Or you won't see any leaves,
Do you know what you're doing to planet Earth?

Adam Baker (11)
Lutley Primary School, Halesowen

Save Our World!

Just make the world a better place
It will put a smile on your face
Lots of things we can do
Lots of things we do new
So please help our world just in case.

Do not leave rubbish on the floor
And buy poppies to help those who fought in the war
They help us when we are scared
Give thanks for what they have shared
So go and try to give the world more.

Charities such as Red Nose Day,
Give it a try and have your say
Men and women go to war
But this won't happen anymore, that's for sure,
Stop it happening, speak up, have your say.

Megan Willetts (11)
Lutley Primary School, Halesowen

Save The Planet

Poison frogs going away,
Time to help them stay.

They help the hunters poison their bow,
But making animals extinct, oh no!

Don't let the rainforest disappear
Because our children won't see the beautiful things out here.

The war is making a really big fuss,
Why don't they sit down, it's time to discuss.

People have debates to have their own way
A person needs to stand up and say

Save the planet!

Daniel Jennings (10)
Lutley Primary School, Halesowen

Save The Planet . . .

Fairtrade products help the poor,
Also help many more.
Try your best to make it fair,
For these people, always care.

Animals lose their habitats,
All of them including cats.
Extinct they will become,
We will only be left with some.

Save our planet and our trees,
All of them with fresh green leaves.
Just work together with relief,
We need to have some belief.

Laura Humphries (11)
Lutley Primary School, Halesowen

Save Our World!

The world won't be a happy place
If we cover it up with such a disgrace,
All the litter on the ground,
The cars polluting and the sound,
Leaving out flammables,
Killing many animals.

Showing our appreciation,
All across the nation,
For the many plants,
It's time to make a stance,
Come on let's not be mean,
Help to make the world green.

Katie Parton (10)
Lutley Primary School, Halesowen

Stop The War And Start The Charity!

There should be a law
That there is no war
They fight for us
So they're not a wuss
They're so brave
So we should all behave.

They do such a good job
So the trees are what you should not rob
Pudsey is a bear
So send some clothes and be fair
Please don't let people go
So say no!

Sam Jones (10)
Lutley Primary School, Halesowen

I'm A Landfill

I am a toy, broken and battered,
I am a lampshade, shading for rats,
I am a pair of sunglasses in the sun,
Rubbish is all I can see.
I am a tin on the floor,
I am a core waiting to be found,
I am a bag hovering all around.
Look at me broken on the ground,
Rubbish is all I can see
Think, put me in a recycling bin.

George Tavernor (9)
Norton-in-Hales CE Primary School, Market Drayton

Litter, Litter, Everywhere

Litter, litter, really bad
The sight of landfills makes me sad
I am determined to sort it out.

Litter, litter, everywhere
What are we going to do here and there?
I am determined to sort it out.

Litter, litter, here and there
How are we going to get there?
It's time to show that we do care!

Bethany Horne (9)
Norton-in-Hales CE Primary School, Market Drayton

Litter, Litter Everywhere

Litter! Litter! Everywhere
Litter! Litter! Over there
Litter! Litter! We need to care
Save the planet, that we share.

Tidy! Tidy! It's all clean
Tidy! Tidy! We are keen
Tidy! Tidy! It's not smelly
Tidy! Tidy! We don't need our wellies.

Sorcha Neill (8)
Norton-in-Hales CE Primary School, Market Drayton

Don't Throw Me Away

Don't throw me away,
You will need me another day.
I can carry your shopping.
I can carry your food,
I can be recycled and used again,
Don't let me end up in a drain.

What am I?
I'm a plastic bag.

Lewis McDonald (7)
Norton-in-Hales CE Primary School, Market Drayton

Litter, Litter

Litter, litter on the floor
Litter, litter on the shore
Litter, litter in the air,
Litter, litter, just everywhere.

Litter, litter on the ground
Litter, litter all around
Litter, litter, do not drop it
Put it in the bin and do your bit!

Lydia Cliffe (8)
Norton-in-Hales CE Primary School, Market Drayton

Recycle

Smelly
Stinky, smoky
I hate it
Recycle, recycle, recycle,
Please!

Jessica Tong (7)
Norton-in-Hales CE Primary School, Market Drayton

Litter, Litter

Litter, litter, stinky things
Litter, litter, cans and tins
Litter, litter, come with me
I am litter, recycle me.

Litter, litter, thrown away
Litter, litter, here I say
Litter, litter, come with me
Litter, litter, recycle me.

Kitty Lambert (7)
Norton-in-Hales CE Primary School, Market Drayton

I Am A Load Of Rubbish

I am a bag zooming in the wind,
I am a bottle rolling by the bin,
I am a crisp packet getting run over,
I am a tin rolling to the shore of Dover.
Litter, litter everywhere
Stop this, it is not fair
We can do much better, but we do not care.

Owen Lloyd (8)
Norton-in-Hales CE Primary School, Market Drayton

Litter, Litter

I am a tin lying on the ground,
I am a crisp packet blowing all around,
I am a bottle floating to the shore,
I am a jam jar smashing on the floor,
Reduce, reuse, recycle because
No one wants a landfill right outside their door!

James McClelland (8)
Norton-in-Hales CE Primary School, Market Drayton

I'm Sick Of Litter

Litter, litter, everywhere
Litter, litter, crashing in my hair
Litter, litter, messing up the air
Litter, litter, it's just everywhere
Litter, litter, in my way
Litter, litter, in the trees
I'm sick of litter, get rid of it all!

Henry Smith (8)
Norton-in-Hales CE Primary School, Market Drayton

Don't Fill Your Bin

Stop the waste, don't fill your bin
Find something else to put it in.
Bottles, cans, yoghurt pots,
You should recycle lots and lots.
Here we go, not in the bin
If you recycle, we will win!

Eleanor Bradeley (8)
Norton-in-Hales CE Primary School, Market Drayton

Here, There, Everywhere

Litter, litter everywhere,
Loads of people think it's unfair
Litter, litter, pongy stuff
Everybody's had enough
Litter, litter goes her and there
You're just not taking care of the planet which we share.

Mae Brennan (7)
Norton-in-Hales CE Primary School, Market Drayton

The Lonely Bag

I am an empty bag, no one wants to use
I'm blowing in the hard wind crying
So sad, trying to stop flying
Worried I will crash into a car or a wall
It is a horrible day,
Why didn't you put me safely away?

Thomas Healey (7)
Norton-in-Hales CE Primary School, Market Drayton

I Am A . . .

I am a bottle falling on the floor
I am a bag floating to the shore
I am a television thrown away
I am a can used for one day
I am a jar of curry
I am going to be recycled, hurry! Hurry!

Connor Bentley (7)
Norton-in-Hales CE Primary School, Market Drayton

Recycle Every Day

R euse cardboard boxes and make them into robots
E mpty your plastic bottles before you recycle them - please
C lose down your PS2 every time you stop using it
Y es we should recycle every day - and night
C ount the number of photocopies - teachers
L ights should be turned off when you leave the room - and when it is light
E veryone should start doing their bit - *now!*

Recycle!

Reece Gairy (10)
Old Oak Primary School, London

The River

I went to the river, and this is what I saw . . .
Water that was stagnant
That did not move
Like a dead snake.
Oil in the water
That tried to trick you
Because it was pretty
Like a butterfly
But it was poisoned water.
A huge inflated thing
In the water.
The place was poor
It looked like the Devil's home.

I went to the river and this is what I thought . . .
What a beautiful place
Turned into an ugly place
What will people think if they come to visit this place?
What will the children do if they touch the poisonous oil?
How did the oil get there?

I went to the river and this is what I saw . . .
Children cleaning the water
Scientists in a shiver
Trying to figure out what was in the river
Is it poisoned oil?
Factories cleaning the bottom of the river
Three days later . . .

It changed colour
From an ugly brown to a beautiful crystal light blue
The fish came swimming back
Then a beautiful sign went up saying, *'No dumping!'*

Ahmed Asad (10)
Old Oak Primary School, London

Let's Think About Our World

Have you ever thought,
How much you throw away?
Have you ever thought,
How much you save every day?
If we work together, and trust me this is true,
We can save our planet,
Just think, me and you!

You know this world we live in,
Do you think it's fine?
Do we keep this world dirty,
Or do we make it shine?
If you understand what I am trying to say,
Would you pick up the rubbish
That other people throw away?
Keep the world tidy and clean
Or keep it smelly with rats,
Which one do you think is better?
The good one or the bad?

Kausar Saeedi (10)
Old Oak Primary School, London

What Can I Do?

R ecycle what you can
E lectricity will run out, so
C hange a light bulb and see what you can save
Y ou can reduce, reuse, recycle every day
C ycling is better for you and makes no pollution
L itter is spreading so look for a bin
I nformation is available at your local council
N ature is disappearing so protect your local parks
G o and start today, every small action makes a difference.

Madlina Haziraj (10)
Old Oak Primary School, London

A Recipe For A Greener World

1 Enthusiastic people
2 Determination
3 Recycled bags
4 Organic food
5 Bottle banks.

Method:
1 Pick up your litter
2 Turn off the taps
3 Switch off the lights
4 Do your washing twice a week, not every day
5 Switch off your TV
6 Do not throw away your chewing gum on the floor
7 Reuse plastic bags
8 Reuse cans and bottles
9 Spread the word!

Asma Zaglam (10)
Old Oak Primary School, London

Environment

E is for environment, there is something we can do
N is for a nice world for me and you
V ery polluted everywhere and . . .
I really think you care
R ecycling is something we can do
O ur world is counting on you
N ow I think you have got the clue
M ore and more we throw away
E stimate how much we throw every day
N ow let's change the world
T omorrow will be a new day.

Kearnaye Dunn & Khadija Said (10)
Old Oak Primary School, London

Don't Take Electricity For Granted

We waste electricity all the time
So never leave lights on!
All those offices with lights burning bright at night
Are they really all full of people working late?
What are we going to do?
I know, I'll write a letter . . .
Dear company, you waste a lot of light,
Do you really work at night?
And if you don't
Turn off the lights,
This is not a pretty sight!

Hammam Aboulfath (10)
Old Oak Primary School, London

You Can Help The Human Race

Recycle, reuse, reduce, don't throw it away
The electricity could run out the next day.
If you think about it, you'll never doubt it
Trees are getting cut down, it's unfair
Soon we'll run out of air.
So if you reuse
You can really help the human race
And make the world a better place.
Don't use a car, the world won't go far
So go on your bike,
If you don't take a hike!

Xenral Imiuru (9)
Old Oak Primary School, London

Recycling Madness

R ecycle what you can
E verything helps
C ontrol the world's future
Y ou can make a difference
C ollect your bags and use them again
L ittle things could help, like recycling paper
E nd the world's crisis!

Moustafa Katamesh (10)
Old Oak Primary School, London

Recycling

R euse your plastic bottles
E very day stop using too much water by turning the tap off
C ould you stop using too much electricity?
Y es it's good to recycle so you can make the world better
C ould you join us today and save the planet?
L et us cut your electricity bills in half
E nd the environment chaos today with us.

Ryan Jones (10)
Old Oak Primary School, London

A Better World - Haiku

Recycle litter
Don't drop it onto the ground.
Make the world better.

Joshua Parr (10)
Rogiet Primary School, Rogiet

If They Can Do It

All around the world
I bet you don't know
What's happening!
The lions are waiting for the recycling van
To collect the bones
From last night's meal.

The polar bears are reading their books
Under the light of an energy saving bulb

The sheep are growing their coats
So they can keep warm
Without turning the heating up.

The kangaroos are doing their shopping
With a pouch for life
Instead of a carrier bag.

So, looking at them
If they can do it, so can you.

Lucy Jenkins
Rogiet Primary School, Rogiet

Don't Forget

Don't forget to turn out the light,
Wasting electricity isn't right.
Don't drop litter as it makes a mess,
Put it in a bin as that's the best.
Don't use the car when you can run,
Walking with your friends is a lot more fun!
Remember to reduce, reuse and recycle every day,
As the world is a better place if kept that way.

Josh Carron (9)
Rogiet Primary School, Rogiet

Making The World A Better Place

Don't take the car to the shops
Let the fumes drop,
Take your bike and ride with pride
Give yourself peace of mind.

Recycle bottles, plastics, tins and papers,
I am sure we'll be grateful later.
Make the world a better place, don't let crime be in its prime
Let us have peace of mind.

Let us breathe in fresh air so forget about lighting fires
And burning those tyres, let the trees blossom.

Let the world be pollution-free
So the air we breathe in can be clean and free.

Sinead Little (9)
Rogiet Primary School, Rogiet

Recycle

Recycle and reuse
That's what's best for you,
They say that on the news
Your rubbish will be something new.

Milk bottles and plastic
Will be made into something fantastic.
Cardboard boxes and paper,
Will make the world a lot safer.

Worms galore, love garden waste,
They have never had a better taste.
Please recycle all your carrier bags,
All cans and all your old mags.

Connor Kington
Rogiet Primary School, Rogiet

World Issues

Plastic, card, paper and glass,
All these things you can recycle.
Garden waste such as twigs or grass,
Food waste, cans and clothes.

There's lots of litter on the floor
Dropping litter is not fun
We've got Earth to care for
Bins are to be used, not to be ignored.

Cars, lorries and motorbikes
All need fuel that pollutes the air
Pollution could make global warming worse
It gets so hot - people want to pull out their hair.

Chloe Knight (9)
Rogiet Primary School, Rogiet

Eco Poem

The land was green
The sea was blue
God made the world great
For me and you
All you have to do
Is your bit
So we can keep this great world fit
Recycle paper
Walk to school
Pick up litter
You're eco cool!

Sophie Powell (9)
Rogiet Primary School, Rogiet

Start Right Now!

Everyone tries to recycle all around the world
And we know that because we do it too.
Because we stick together when we do something
Hey, remember it's for all of us not just for you.
Are you recycling?
Well if you're not
Start right now!
To help everyone, start now!

Alice Davies (9)
Rogiet Primary School, Rogiet

Why?

Why does war have to happen?
Why do millions of people die every day?
Why can't people see this?
Why are we horrible to each other?
Why are we mean?
Because we are at war about people being different.
Why are we angry?
Because people at war want to be best.
Why are we selfish?
Because we don't think of anyone else.
Why are we greedy?
Because we are taking more than we need.
Why are we nasty?
Because people don't care about each other.
Why do we let this happen?
Why can't people treat each other the same?
Why can't we love each other?
Why?

Tonicha Luffman (10)
St David's RC Primary School, Newport

Deforestation

D on't cut down trees
E veryone can do their bit
F orests are for animals
O ur future depends on oxygen
R eplant trees if you cut them down
E co-team
S ave the environment
T ell people not to cut down trees
A nimals are suffering
T rees keep birds and monkeys safe
I want to save the trees
O ur animals depend on us
N o cutting our trees!

Regan Crockett (7)
St David's RC Primary School, Newport

Wicked War

War brings sadness, unhappiness and fear
Make sure you listen and you hear
Those people who ask you to stop.
War brings death and murder
But also the colour bright red.
Think of all those people
Who were innocent but now are dead.
People killing people, it's not a pretty sight,
Guns go *flash*, bombs go *bang*
All day and all night.
Help stop war wherever you are
And make the world a safe and happy place.

Elisabeth Williams (10)
St David's RC Primary School, Newport

Recycling To Save Our World

Paper, card, tin cans and bottles that are plastic,
Recycling them to be made into something new is really fantastic.
Our Earth is something special and we need to look after it.
Just by recycling we're doing our bit.
If we don't recycle, we'll fill up our land.
Me personally, I think this should be banned.
As you might know our trees give us oxygen
And they are beautiful nature.
If we cut down our trees then we'll have less oxygen
And no pretty trees to look at.

Think before you act, don't destroy our world!

Hannah Price (10)
St David's RC Primary School, Newport

War

Think of the people who die every day,
Just because of people who like it.
War is people screaming for their lives,
War is people with angry faces,
War is people who have bravery to fight,
War is innocent people and children dying.
War is dirt and mud everywhere,
You should stop war right now.
There are fires and bombs and guns
And soon there will be nothing left to see!

Bethan Davidge (10)
St David's RC Primary School, Newport

Help Us!

Deforestation will destroy our planet.
Stop cutting down trees please!
Leave the monkeys' homes there.
The poor things have nowhere to live.
You might be giving us paper
But we are losing our oxygen.
The monkeys are dying because of you
I love monkeys, don't you?
Help us please!

Grace Hurley (8)
St David's RC Primary School, Newport

What Is Pollution?

P oor little fish and
O ther species
L iving in the
L itter-filled water.
U rgh, litter in the water
T errible, water species dying.
I f you will help to stop pollution, fish and
O ther water species will
N ever live in polluted water again!

Luc Taran Joseff Simmonds (8)
St David's RC Primary School, Newport

War

If we don't stop this, people will be sad.
War is unhappy faces.
War is green and red.
War is death.
War is people running.
War is danger.
War is people screaming in fear.
If this is stopped,
People would be happy and feel safe in this world.

Jessica Nightingale (10)
St David's RC Primary School, Newport

Recycle

R emember to recycle,
E verybody should
C lap your hand and everyone would
Y ou can help too
C ome on people of the world,
L et it be a better place
E veryone recycle. Reduce, reuse, recycle
　　Recycle green to keep it clean.

Carys Parselle (8)
St David's RC Primary School, Newport

Recycle, Recycle

Don't be a litterbug with rubbish on the floor
Keep the city tidy, we don't want it anymore.
Recycle tins, don't put them in the bins,
Recycle boxes to help the foxes.
Recycle cans and the world won't be sad.

Megan Hughes (9)
St David's RC Primary School, Newport

Our World

Our world is precious,
But is being destroyed by people like us.
We need to save it,
Bit by bit.
Littering and pollution has to stop.
Lose its fizz like a bottle of pop.
War must stop too,
But to do it, we need help from you!

Ffion Joseph (10)
St David's RC Primary School, Newport

Do Our Bit

B ecome responsible
E nvironmentally friendly

G reen is the colour to help save our planet,
R ecycle now, save resources,
E nergy-saving devices, help save the world,
E co-friendly products can reduce pollution,
N ow we all need to do our bit.

William Ryley (10)
St David's RC Primary School, Newport

Green Box

Plastic and glass bottles,
Yoghurt pots and metal tins,
You can recycle all sorts of things.
So protect our planet;
Use your green box and can it!

Ieuan Matthews (8)
St David's RC Primary School, Newport

Recycle

R euse paper, glass, plastic and bottles
E njoy recycling, it could be fun
C an you do it?
Y es you can do it, everyone can recycle
C ome on start recycling
L et's start recycling now
E veryone put your bit in the recycling bin.

Mollie Joseph (7)
St David's RC Primary School, Newport

Recycle

R ecycle your litter and don't be bitter.
E veryone can help us recycle.
C an you help us too?
Y ou can do it!
C ans can be recycled too.
L itter is very bad if you put it on the floor.
E veryone can do their bit.

Jordan Lois Ingles (8)
St David's RC Primary School, Newport

Recycle, Recycle

R emember to recycle rubbish.
E co-friendly.
C ans can be recycled more.
Y ou can help us recycle more.
C ans can be crushed.
L et's recycle eco-friends.
E veryone recycle more and more.

Niall Graham (8)
St David's RC Primary School, Newport

Recycle

R ecycle your rubbish when you are done
E at all your food, don't waste
C ans and tins can be recycled too
Y ou can help us recycle
C ans can be recycled over and over again
L itter is bad if you put it on the floor
E co-people, help us out!

Georgia Hillman (9)
St David's RC Primary School, Newport

Help The World

R euse all things if possible
E veryone can make a difference
C an you make the world a better place to live in?
Y ou have a job to do, now go out there and do it!
C an you help?
L ove the world
E veryone please help.

Kevin Sunil (8)
St David's RC Primary School, Newport

Recycle With Us

R ecycle things like plastic, paper and glass.
E veryone can recycle, even you!
C ans and bottles can be recycled too.
Y ou can get a recycling bin.
C ould you help?
L ots of things go in the recycling bin.
E veryone can recycle, help us do it!

Elinor Davies (7)
St David's RC Primary School, Newport

Care For Our World

R euse plastic, cans and paper.
E veryone can recycle!
C ans can be recycled.
Y ou can look after your world by recycling.
C are for your world.
L ook out for paper and recycle it.
E veryone can look after the world by recycling.

Emily Friel (8)
St David's RC Primary School, Newport

Recycle, Reuse, Reduce

R ecycle, reuse, reduce
E veryone can help
C reate a world of
Y our own where everyone
C an help
L et's go and tell
E veryone, you can help too!

Evie Bignell (8)
St David's RC Primary School, Newport

Recycle

R ecycle cans, plastic and paper.
E veryone needs to do it.
C ans can be recycled too.
Y ou can do it!
C ome and recycle with us.
L et's reuse plastic, paper and glass.
E veryone can do it, so come on let's recycle!

Erin Bryony Martin (7)
St David's RC Primary School, Newport

Recycle, Recycle

R ecycle old objects
E veryone can help us out
C ardboard can be recycled
Y ou can do it too
C ans are good to use, so don't throw them on the floor
L itter should never be thrown on the floor, put it in the bin!
E veryone can do it, great!

Sinead Davison (8)
St David's RC Primary School, Newport

Global Warming, Wasting Paper, Electricity

Global warming

Global warming is definitely not cool
So help us out
Don't be a fool.

Don't just sit around
Stop the global warming now!

Wasting paper

Please don't waste paper
Trees are becoming rarer.

The rarer they get
The more animals will have to visit the vet!

Electricity

Please don't waste electricity
Because we want to save the city.

We need our city
If we lose it, that's a pity!

Heather MacNeil
St John's Primary School, Barrhead

Be Kind To The Earth

Be kind to the Earth
Don't be a litterbug
If everyone stops
We won't even fill half a jug.

Global warming isn't hard to understand,
If everyone gives a helping hand
Just turn off a light
And everything will be right.

Unfortunate to say
Our world is becoming a dump.
Please recycle
And we won't have a big rubbish lump.

Graffiti and vandalism isn't the way,
Our world needs help by the day,
The Earth is starting to bend,
Life might not end,
If the Earth is your friend.

Don't murder the Earth,
Stop the pollution!
Don't use the car
Help this solution.

Don't cut down trees,
Keep them alive,
If you do,
We'll get enough oxygen
Then we will survive.

Don't be a fool,
Please follow these rules,
If you do,
You are cool.
Be environmentally friendly.

Chloe O'Hara
St John's Primary School, Barrhead

The Litterbug

Don't drop litter,
Don't be a fool,
Save our planet
And you will be cool!

Don't drop litter over our planet,
Save our world from the litterbug.
We all drop litter once in a while
But stop it now!

Most people don't care,
But if this happens it will look like a dump.
Once my school made a sign
It said, 'Stop it now. It's been too long!'

Children grow up here,
In this smelly dump.
Make it happier for them.
It would be nice if we stopped,
But how?

Please don't litter,
I can't bear it.
Walking through it in the morning,
It's like walking through a commotion,
It's like a polluted ocean.

You might be chuffed,
But when we see it we huff.
Why do it? It's disgusting,
Stop it now!

This is an enormous dump,
What do you think of it?
Every morning I look out the window
And see litter
Stop it now. It's wrong!

Caitlin Curran (10)
St John's Primary School, Barrhead

Mother Nature

Mother Nature needs a rest
So let's all try and do our best.

Oh everyone stop throwing litter about
It makes people very sad.
Oh, I almost forgot,
It's very bad!

This is not right,
 It hurts our planet in every way,
Just do something small every day.

Help stop the litterbugs,
Don't just sit there with a mug.

Every day you will see a car,
Don't always drive, even though it's far.

Recycle every day if you can,
Don't be a fool, man.

Never drop litter
That would be bitter.

A litterbug is bad
Please don't do it,
It makes people sad.

Trees are dying
And everyone is crying.

Unfortunately we are breaking the ozone layer
Because there are cars here and there.

Rabbits and squirrels are losing their homes,
They will have to hide inside garden gnomes.

Eventually everything will be right.
The sky will give us lots of light.

Erin Cassidy (8)
St John's Primary School, Barrhead

Litter World

Don't drop litter,
Don't be a fool!
Don't drop litter,
It's so not cool!

In one way litter is a crime.
Remember the Earth is not just yours or mine.
I think litter is very bad
And it can make the council very sad.

We try to pick it up.
I know we do.
We try to pick it up
Tell the truth, do you?

Our environment is in such a state.
If you see someone dropping litter
Say, 'Hey mate, don't be so bitter!'

Our Earth is in a mess,
This world is in a dreadful stress.
Some people think, *I don't care*
But actually I say, 'Don't you dare!'

Litter is so dreadfully shocking!
Some people drop litter while they are talking.
If you don't drop litter you will be a magician!
But if you do, the world will be in a worse position.

All of this world is in your hands,
Not to litter would be one of God's ten commands.
So remember save litter,
And don't be so bitter!

Holly Harris
St John's Primary School, Barrhead

Save Our Nature

Save our environment,
Don't cut down trees,
Don't waste paper,
Or you won't see lovely leaves!

If you don't save the environment,
You won't see green grass,
You'll be very sad,
You'll be crass.

Please, please, please be fair,
You won't have to share,
And you won't care.

So don't be slow
Or the world will go low.

If you don't see the light
You won't shine bright.
Please don't cry,
Just give it a try.

People will see who you really are
Instead of a lump of tar.

So now you know what to do.
Don't be sad.
Just do what I do!

Lauren McGuire (10)
St John's Primary School, Barrhead

Eco Poem

Global warming is becoming a disgrace,
Getting worse at a rapid pace.
The Earth is coming to an end,
We need help from you and your friends.

If you are in the house resting on a cushion,
You should be helping clear the pollution.
We need you to show you care,
This is affecting the ozone layer.

Don't sit drinking from some mugs,
Stop those litterbugs!
Put your litter in a bin
And fish won't lose a fin!

If you throw anything
It will look minging.
If you litter, you should have sorrow,
If you don't stop, it will be the same tomorrow.

We are getting a bad atmosphere,
We need help from you and your peers.
Stick to the rule,
Don't be cruel!

Hannah Coyle
St John's Primary School, Barrhead

Eco Poem

E arth will melt if we
A re not careful
R ising temperatures
T hat are scorching
H ot, hot, hot!

Jodie Robb (9)
St John's Primary School, Barrhead

Save Energy

Save energy, turn off lights,
Turn off heating, put on some tights.
Don't put so much petrol in your car
Then the world will obviously go far.

Walk to school, don't take the bus!
If you walk to school there will be no fuss.
Don't sit on the couch and watch TV.
So come on up and save energy.

When we have saved energy,
Then this world will never be at sea.
When this world is saved
Even more children will be made.

Our world keeps complaining
Only turn on lights when it's raining.
Let's make this world a better place,
Don't you want to see children with a smiley face?

Do you want to save energy?
If you do then,
You will be a champion too!

Carly Bremner (10)
St John's Primary School, Barrhead

Go Green!

Global warming is so bad
It will make the world sad.

Litter, gas, all the rest,
People who waste it are nasty pests.

Please Mother Nature have a rest
Because everyone will try their best.

Graffiti and vandalism are spoiling our world
It's really bad, it makes us sad.

Animals' habitats are being destroyed
If we stop they will get them back.

Don't waste your food and drink
Please think, please.

Please don't waste paper
Then it won't destroy the animals' habitats.

Please don't use the car, and recycle
Would it hurt if you could cycle?

Jack Phillips (9)
St John's Primary School, Barrhead

Eco Poem

Litter is getting us into a mess,
The people are getting depressed.
The Earth is coming under destruction,
We need to get it right and start reconstruction.

Global warming is so sad,
Try to help out and be a good lad.
Don't be a fool and turn off plugs,
You are not a lazy slug.

Kevin Walsh (9)
St John's Primary School, Barrhead

Litter Poem

Litter is disgusting, smelly and wrong.
Everyone does it.
It won't be on for too long.
But I do care, I can't bear it.

It's making the world horrible.
It will become a big trash can.
I want a better world,
What about you?

It will be beautiful,
Make it happy for children
To grow up in.
It was happy for adults, why not us?

Make it happy and beautiful,
It was beautiful but now it's better!
Stop it now if you want a better world
Some people do. What about you?

Don't litter!

Emily Docherty (10)
St John's Primary School, Barrhead

Stop Pollution

We all pollute in different ways,
Most people don't care.
It will change the seas, the days,
But who would dare?

We all see it in different emotions,
It's sad for the fish that swim around.
You won't see sharks swimming in the oceans,
If you do, the fish will drop with a pound.

We can put up a sign,
That says 'Don't pollute seas'.
If we do, the world will shine,
And we will have more fish on which to dine.

Don't put oil in the seas,
It's really not nice.
There will be an injury,
And fish will become hard as ice.

Kyle Johnston (10)
St John's Primary School, Barrhead

Eco Poem

Imagine what it would be like,
If no cars were on the street,
The streets were shiny clean,
There would be no litter at your feet

If the whole of Africa,
Got covered in desert sand,
It would be a dry terrain,
So give a helping hand

The world is soon going to end,
I am so despondent,
I might put out some letters,
And hope people respond to it

Greenhouse gases are very bad,
If there is a heatwave it will be so roasting that
The ice caps may melt,
And the penguins and polar bears will not have a habitat.

Rachel Hughes
St John's Primary School, Barrhead

Mother Nature Poem

The planet is coming to an end
And the only way to stop is to be the Earth's friend.

The ozone layer is coming to demise
We must stop it before everyone cries.

Litter is everywhere and there's nowhere to play
This is boring in every way.

Mother Nature can't do it all
Let's go for it and get on the ball.

I don't know why everyone is wasting paper
Stop it now, or give Mother Nature more labour.

Don't be a fool
If you want the Earth to stay cool.

There is only one more thing I have to say
Let's recycle and do it today!

Adam Canning (9)
St John's Primary School, Barrhead

Mother Nature Is Hurt

Global warming is destroying our planet
So let's help each other and together we can stop it.

This is our Earth, we must try to save it.
So let's turn off power and save electricity.

The sun is coming through and we won't get away
Unless we start trying today, today, today!

This is our planet, we must save it right now,
Let's help our planet before we take a bow.

This is pathetic, the temperatures are outstandingly high,
So don't stop there, try, try, try!

Aidan McGuigan (9)
St John's Primary School, Barrhead

Save Energy

Save energy, walk to school
And in the future you'll be cool!
Don't use your car so much,
And you'll have a lot of luck.

Save energy every day,
And in the morning you'll be blasting away!
If you turn your radiator down,
It may be cold, but grab a jumper and go into town!

If you don't turn your TV off at night,
Flames will be blaring oh so bright.
In the morning when you go out to school,
Turn your lights off and be so cool!

Save energy and be cool!

Erin Shankland (10)
St John's Primary School, Barrhead

Eco Poem

M ust stop now!
O r else the world will howl.
T orture will beat the Earth,
H ow will pollution stop?
E arth is coming to an end,
R abbits and others will lose their homes.

N ever drop litter
A nd
T ell everyone to pick it up.
U nfortunately people use cars
R evolution can be our friend if
E arth is going to end.

Carmen Cassidy
St John's Primary School, Barrhead

Mother Nature

M other Nature
O ur world is dying
T oday we all will be trying
H elp us change our ways
E veryone united to save our world today
R ound and round our world spins

N ew things every day
A desert overgrowing is something really bad
T o make this stop everyone take a part
U sed to sunshine or rain, it's so confusing is it not?
R un now, tell the news, everyone; we're counting on you
E veryone do your part, help us now.

Anna Campbell (9)
St John's Primary School, Barrhead

Recycle For A Future

Recycle for a life, a tomorrow, a future.

Avoid a world full of rubbish,
A world where no one smiles,
And where there's no chance of laughter.

Avoid a world full of methane,
A world where no children are happy,
And where you always see frowns.

Create a world full of cleanliness,
A world where everyone smiles,
And where all you hear is laughter.

Recycle for a life, a tomorrow, a future.

Caitlin Feeney-Miles (9)
Shinewater Primary School, Eastbourne

Landfill

A starving goblin,
Chomping and munching
At the rubbish we throw.
A giant's armchair
Made out of disgusting rubbish.
Each piece of rubbish we throw away
Pollutes the planet more every year.
Recycle even more.
We can save the planet
For everyone to live!

William Carter (9)
Shinewater Primary School, Eastbourne

Landfill

A huge monster
Eating all of our rubbish.
If you feed him he will soon overflow
And more and more rubbish will soon get too high,
And all you will see in the distance
Will be a mountain of rubbish.
Then there will be no room left for us.

James Bezant (10)
Shinewater Primary School, Eastbourne

Landfill

A hungry monster
Waiting for your rubbish.
Do not feed her
For she could destroy the world.

Chloe Edgar-Connell (9)
Shinewater Primary School, Eastbourne

Landfill

A hungry troll
Eating everything near,
Waiting for more every day,
His sharp teeth
Biting into your rubbish.
Do not feed him!

Leanna Rebaudo (10)
Shinewater Primary School, Eastbourne

War!

Walking, marching, running for the trenches,
Bodies, bodies, bodies, bodies.
What have we done?
We've caused total chaos.

Three, two, one . . . *fire!*
Blast! Boom! Bang!
Sirens of evacuation pierce my ears.
Bombardment is underway!
Capture is the objective!
Guarding paratroopers protect their territory.
Running for our lives,
Falling deeper as we feel constant pain and fail to carry on
Stairs of light appear
I climb higher and higher and reach it
I fade away within the gushes of the wind.
Before you know it, I'm awake!
But this time I'm dead . . .
Gushing through Flanders fields as invisible as can be
Flashback, after flashback, after flashback!

Luke Russell (11)
Stroud Green Primary School, London

So Much Fighting

War is such a disaster,
People dying all the time.
We invade the space of
Iran, Iraq and Afghanistan.
Bullets thrust through their hopes and dreams,
They stay awake and cry.

Parents have mental breakdowns,
Protecting their families' lives,
Whilst praying to the Lord
Wrapped up in their blankets.
Air raids destroying their houses,
Destruction living around them.

They have nowhere to go,
They have nowhere to run,
They flee to the nearest safe spot,
And stay there throughout their lives.
There is nothing much we can do,
But show that we care.

Kofi Odoom (10)
Stroud Green Primary School, London

Help Our Rainforest

Animals and people dying
Because people keep cutting down our rainforests.
If anyone in the world could stop them
It could be you.
This makes me feel so angry.
I know it's not just me that feels this way.
So please, please recycle your paper
So we can stop cutting down the rainforest trees.
This needs to stop!

Shyante Bucknor
Stroud Green Primary School, London

War

War! Why does war have to be?
There is no point in war.
People getting killed,
Saving their country.
If only I had a magic wand
To make the world a better place.
War! War!
It is like a lot of brothers killing each other.
Why can't people just get along?
If only I had a magic wand.
Life is too short for war,
Kids are getting killed.
Why does there have to be war.
It does not matter how old you are
You should still not get killed.

Isaac Asher Bracey (10)
Stroud Green Primary School, London

War

War is against us that is true,
Some people listen, the others never do.
Nations fight but it's not right,
Forgive and forget, that's the light.
Mothers are crying, people are dying
And they are trying but it's no use
Obviously they can't choose.
Bombs are spreading everywhere
Evacuations happening anywhere.
Diseases continuing each and every day
What do people think about it?
It's your turn to say.

Koos Osman (11)
Stroud Green Primary School, London

War Is Evil

War is chaos, war is evil,
War causes us to die inside.
If we could make peace
We wouldn't die inside.
If we don't - instant death!
Why not peace?
Why not say yes?
You have been blinded,
Blinded by rage
By hate also
By death.
That is the meaning of war
We must stop it
At all costs
We must stop!

Joel Falconer (9)
Stroud Green Primary School, London

The Rainforest

The rainforest has millions of trees,
Now they're starting to decrease.
So stop cutting the trees
And let us breathe
Some . . . oxygen.

Paper comes from trees,
Well, you must know that
But if you recycle
You never know
You could be using
The same one!

Nesrine Benaouda (10)
Stroud Green Primary School, London

Untitled

What happened to the environment?
What happened to the environment?
Why are the streets so disgusting?
Because we drive cars,
We're destroying our world.
Take care of our environment.
I say stop polluting the air now!
But they won't listen to me.
So now I am angry, more than ever
So I decide we need to do something about it.

First, be dominant, clean up the streets,
Second, recycle cans, bottles and glasses,
Don't drive lorries and cars
And that will make a cleaner environment.

Afia Headley (10)
Stroud Green Primary School, London

Cheetah

It has the finest essential fur that has the colour of a yellow shard,
With its long, firm, balanced tail, it has defeated many enemies.
With its speed and glowing eyes, wide open, looking for prey . . .
It strikes!
With a powerful hit from its colossal furry paw.
The cheetah!

The cheetah lashes at its foes with its razor-sharp teeth,
Its spots as black as the night, help it to camouflage
in the green grass.
Then it slashes an ox with its sharp claws, killing its prey
with no mercy.
Sadly it is close to extinction.
The cheetah!

Léo Bouniol (10)
Stroud Green Primary School, London

Litter

You use me,
You don't give me a second chance,
You could have put me in the recycling bin,
It was just there.
Instead you put me in the worst possible place,
The black bin!
Not that black bin, it can't be.
I get chucked in that smelly place you call a truck,
There is loads of me in there.
Then we get here,
The landfill site.
I deserve better than this,
I am litter,
Recyclable!

Harry Thurlow (11)
Stroud Green Primary School, London

Pollution

Pollution.
It's vile,
It's disgusting
And we need to stop it.
Instead of fiendish driving,
You could ride your bike.
Turning off energy-swallowing lights also helps.
You could ride on the bus
Instead of driving.
All these thoughtful things,
Will put an end to loathsome pollution.

Ezra Glasstone (10)
Stroud Green Primary School, London

Problems And Answers

Pollution's eliminating us,
Pollution's exterminating us.
Solar power is the way of the future.
Solar power is loveable and kind.
Littering is killing animals,
Littering is destroying us.
Love is helping and understanding,
Love is helping us.
We can defeat litter,
We can defeat pollution,
But most importantly, we can make peace.

Tommy Peter Heintz (9)
Stroud Green Primary School, London

Litter

Look how dangerous litter is,
People can catch diseases,
You can smell the smelly roads,
It comes to the top of your nose.

Litter can kill animals,
All the litter bins are full,
Someone needs to make it better
And they could do it with a litter picker.

Everyone, we're on our knees
Pleading, 'Take away the litter, please!'

Senanur Duven (9)
Stroud Green Primary School, London

When I Come Out Of School

When I come out of school,
I see (of course you),
Trees as green as an emerald velvet dress,
Flowers as mellow as fruit,
People as ecstatic as can be.

But what I don't want to see is . . .
A hole in the ozone layer and . . .
Piles of rubbish,
Buildings as tall as Mount Everest,
Birds as dead as can be!

Joel Milo Robinson (9)
Stroud Green Primary School, London

Going, Going, Gone!

The dodo has already gone,
Many more will follow.
Hunters decrease the numbers,
Nature reserves protect.
All of the endangered
Are controlled in national parks.

All North and South Pole inhabitants,
White rhino and African elephants
Are being killed by both climate change and humans.
Animals are separated, dying in despair.

Leon Brocklehurst (10)
Stroud Green Primary School, London

The Helpful Ghost

The ghost came with the clouds.
He walked the streets of where he used to live when he was alive.
He remembered that the roads were as clean as crystal.
If only you could see them now.
Plastic bags flying around, rubbish all over the place.
The ghost picked up a rubbish picker
And picked up all the rubbish on the road he used to live on
He thought, if he could do this, he could help the world,
So he did and now the world is litter-free and it's time for him to go.

He whispered to the world, 'Don't litter again!'

Reece Thomas (10)
Stroud Green Primary School, London

Recycling

Recycling is so much better than dumping rubbish in landfill.
It is better for the environment.
It is healthier, it can save the Earth.
Earth will get dirty and filthy.

You can reuse it, it is tidier.
If you recycle your recyclables,
The Earth will be much cleaner.
The Earth will be greatly improved.

Zain Hosein (10)
Stroud Green Primary School, London

I Recycle - Haiku

Please do recycle
If you want a happy place,
Recycle today.

Edwina Stewart
Stroud Green Primary School, London

Trees

Killing animals is not good,
Cutting down trees, it isn't right.
When we lose our oxygen
We are going to blame it on you.
When you cut down trees
You are wasting all the paper.
We complain but you don't care.
It is all going to come back on you!

Sharde
Stroud Green Primary School, London

Litter

I feel bitter
When you drop litter.
Cardboard boxes, cans and tins,
Put them in your recycling bins.
Don't throw your litter in the bin,
Or the landfill sites will win.
Animals die and you don't care,
I don't think that is very fair!

Micah Crook (10)
Stroud Green Primary School, London

Litter

Every time you use a tin
You should put it in the bin,
Do not let the landfill win
Or there will be rubbish up to your chin.
Everyone should recycle,
Or we'll banish the animal cycle.

Tony Canli (10)
Stroud Green Primary School, London

Wars Are Bad

When there's a war, the world turns upside down.
There is violence, terror and destruction.
Soon there's blood and deaths.
The world could be blown to bits.
There should be no guns, bombs or war!
There should be happiness in the world
And we could live together in peace.

Daniel Nicholson (9)
Stroud Green Primary School, London

Litter

Litter kills a lot of things
Why do people do it?
They do it because they have nowhere to put it.
Litter is like a scrunched-up piece of paper
Just taking up space.
Litter is like an apple core
Rotting on the dirty floor.

Sebek Sturgeon (9)
Stroud Green Primary School, London

Litter

Litter is what irresponsible humans produce every day.
Every day animals get injured by our litter.
We must stop littering today!
Animals can lose a leg, get their mouths stuck in cans and much more.
So I have one thing to say to you,
'Stop murdering our land! You'll be sorry!'

Adina Grant-Adams (10)
Stroud Green Primary School, London

We Can Make Our World A Better Place

Dirt is fear,
Dirt is something we don't want to see.
Crime is bad it makes me feels like there's crime all around me,
Crime is disgraceful.
Racism is something we don't like to hear,
Racism is sadness,
Together we can make a warm and loving place.

Olubunmi Oyinka Wabessy (9)
Stroud Green Primary School, London

War

If you are in the army you can get killed
And it tears your family apart.
Wars are not good.
People dying, men crying, all because of war.
Homes burning, planes crashing, all because of war.
Children getting hurt, all because of war.
Guns firing, weapons breaking, all because of war.

Aljay Shackeil Wilson (11)
Stroud Green Primary School, London

Litter

You can see it everywhere
Rats, mice, flies and spiders everywhere.
Animals get hurt
Some of the little baby animals get hurt
Because there is so much litter around.
It's not good for the environment.

Leon Dunkley (9)
Stroud Green Primary School, London

Pollution

I we do not do our part to stop polluting the Earth,
It will die and humans will die.
The rivers will turn black,
Tap water will turn black.
Bottles and glass thrown into seas.
Please do you part to help!

Shahzaib Mhamad
Stroud Green Primary School, London

Recycling

Recycling is about people doing their bit for the environment.
Recycling is about getting rid of litter that really smells.
Recycling decreases the dangers of animals dying.
Recycling makes animals and people happy.
So recycle and save the planet!

Cedric Baksh (10)
Stroud Green Primary School, London

War - Haiku

Oh no look at how,
People dying, bombs flying,
Please stop war right now!

Salma Chakour (11)
Stroud Green Primary School, London

A Pollution - Haiku

Pollution is bad
The world is getting hotter
Help us save the world.

Darshan Leslie
Stroud Green Primary School, London

The War - Haiku

War is terrible
People die with no one there
They are near their death.

Yaamin Chowdhury (10)
Stroud Green Primary School, London

Wars - Haiku

Family cry, 'Help!'
Families fight enemies.
Please stop all the wars.

Joshua Agbagidi
Stroud Green Primary School, London

Oil And Litter

Clear silky seas glint warmly in the sun,
Silver shoals of fish finally having fun.
Oil at last gone, no dirty water causing creatures to run,
Free so free, at home again,
No oil spill . . . no stress . . . no pain.

A while ago, a few years or so,
A dark, thick cloud smothered my home,
My heart, my hope, I had to go.
No coral, no seaweed, my lungs just pleading, at last . . .
Free so free, at home again,
No oil spill . . . no stress . . . no pain.

My troop, my shoal, were strong, so bold,
Fighting for survival, we've been there, it's a load.
No fear, we're brave, our pride is true,
Our hope, honest, is that clear to you?
We need your help, your power please,
We can fight through this, just give us your mercy . . .
Free so free, at home again,
No oil spill . . . no stress . . . no pain.

What about us? What about my friends?
Dolphins, whales, extinction is coming - for us it's the end.
The view isn't pretty, once we're dead,
Rotting body parts, you know the rest.

Keep the past in the past, how long will it last?
Our life isn't fair, it's going to fast,
Please, please keep the past in the past.

You can make a difference, you can help the world,
You are our heroes, if you save our peril.

Molly Higgins
Walter Halls Primary School, Mapperley

Pollution, Pollution

Pollution, pollution,
What has it done?
It's taken away all the time and fun.

Pollution, pollution,
Please stop now,
I'll find a solution, for you somehow.

Pollution, pollution,
Time has nearly gone,
I'll stop pollution,
Help everyone.

I've had enough!

Pick up your can off the floor,
Stop throwing bubblegum,
Don't throw anymore.

Carry litter until you find a bin,
Don't chuck it in the lake,
A fish will damage its fin.

Trying to stop it,
Trying to help,
Nothing's happened
It's your turn to try
And say it loud.

Stop pollution!
Stop it now!

Georgia Bird
Walter Halls Primary School, Mapperley

Recycling

If somebody drops rubbish on the ground,
Please don't do it.
The animals will eat it and die.
Put it in the bin.
If somebody drops chewing gum on the ground.
Please don't do it.
It will stick on the shoes.
Put it in the bin.
Recycle plastic and glass.
Please do it.

Recycle cans and papers.
Please do it.
Put the rubbish in the recycle bins now.
Please do it.
Keep the world beautiful.

Amy Rose Perkins (11)
Warton Nethersole's CE Primary School, Warton

Look At Me

Look at me, look at me, I'm so unhappy,
Let me free, let me free!
Stop throwing food in to me,
Let me hunt for my own food.
Put me in a forest, put me in a forest
So I can find my fiancée.
Together we could grow a family,
Together we could live and be free.
I'm a tiger big and fierce,
I can look after myself.
So look at me, and let me free -
Please!

Alfie Apps (10)
Warton Nethersole's CE Primary School, Warton

Rainforest

Where am I?
There are lots of my species around me.
Monkeys are on my branches,
There are clouds above me.
I can hear a rumbling noise.
I know where I am,
Home!
The rainforest.

But the rumbling gets louder,
There is a man cutting down the trees.
He comes to me
Don't do this please, please.

No!

Harry Kilkenny (8)
Warton Nethersole's CE Primary School, Warton

Recycling The World

When the world is turning dull and gloomy
Help is needed.
Recycling is good fun.
If you throw plastic bags on the floor,
Animals will eat them
Please don't do it!
If you chuck your food or sweets on the floor
Other people have to pick up
After millions of germs have been on them.
Put them in the bin, please do it,
Make the world a better place to be.
Use your recycling bins!
You can save the planet.

Chloe Kimberley (10)
Warton Nethersole's CE Primary School, Warton

We Don't Want These Things

We don't want pollution,
We want the world to be green,
So if we all recycle,
We'll all be one big team.

We don't want extinction,
We want wildlife around,
So if we don't litter,
There will be paw prints in the ground.

We don't want any war,
There's nothing much we can do,
We want everyone OK,
So it can be safe for me and you.

Hazelle Whitehead (11)
Warton Nethersole's CE Primary School, Warton

Alone

I am so poor,
Poverty is a bore,
I hate my life.

My future is bare,
My food is rare,
My bones are weak,
I can hardly speak.

This is the end of my life,
Because I am so, so poor.
I really hate my life,
It is such a bore.

Nathan Daniel Worrall (10)
Warton Nethersole's CE Primary School, Warton

Recycle

When the world is turning grey
And you really want to say . . .
Recycle
Make the world a better place
Don't just watch this disgrace.

So when the world is turning blue
And you really want to say . . .
We weren't mean
We were green.
We were fed up of seeing this disgrace
So we made the world a better place.

Charlotte Hopkins (10)
Warton Nethersole's CE Primary School, Warton

Take Action

As the elephants protect their young
They form a wall of iron.
The calf is almost invisible from the outside world.
They protect the calf in a different way to you and me.
The female stays to protect and to guide the calf away.

Why don't we form this wall of protection
For the world and all its nature.
Say no to cars and smoking,
Don't leave these chemicals in the air.
Thank you.

Ian Ryan (9)
Warton Nethersole's CE Primary School, Warton

Save The Animals

Many little animals
Big ones too, have died
Because of us, because of us, it's true.
We need to act now
Before it's too late.

What can we do?
What shall we think?
Think of the animals and how they must feel.
Stop cutting trees down
Stop, stop right now!

Carys Langham (9)
Warton Nethersole's CE Primary School, Warton

Animal Jail

I wonder why I am behind bars
It's horrible.
It's like an animal jail.
Why do they throw food at me?
There's only my wife and me here -
It's horrible.
I want to be free
And hunt for my own food
Not stuck here.
I want to go home!

Jake Allman (10)
Warton Nethersole's CE Primary School, Warton

The Monkey

I was in the zoo one day
When I heard some people say
That monkeys were going away
Never to return again.
I never knew their names
But spotted these men with guns.
They shot my mother and my friend with their guns
And carried them away
Never to be seen again.
Save the monkeys!

Tom Sear (10)
Warton Nethersole's CE Primary School, Warton

Disease

I am very unhealthy,
My face is covered in spots,
I have to live on the streets
With only pans and pots.

The car fumes are making me unhealthy,
I really want them to stop.
If you could stop using cars
It would really help a lot.
Stop polluting the environment!

Joshua Jones (10)
Warton Nethersole's CE Primary School, Warton

Recycling

R ubbish is bad.
E nvironment needs saving.
C ans can be recycled.
Y ou can help the Earth.
C hewing gum litters the pavement.
L itter is bad, put it in the bin!
I f you love animals don't litter.
N ew rulers can be made from plastic cups.
G reen up your life.

Rebekah Ann Harrison (10)
Warton Nethersole's CE Primary School, Warton

Rubbish Dumps

Rubbish dumps, petrol pumps,
Many, many more.
All these things have got to end,
Because the Earth is coming to a bend.
Polar bears, Arctic hares,
All these things will die.
Ice caps melting,
They need helping
Or everything will die.

Owen Langham (9)
Warton Nethersole's CE Primary School, Warton

The Big Green Poetry Machine

The world will be a better place if we,
Recycle and don't kill.
A tank can pollute the atmosphere
So remember, don't be mean, be green!

Edward Baker (10)
Warton Nethersole's CE Primary School, Warton

Crazy Recycle

R ecycling is good for everybody
E ngland can be green
C limate change we don't want
Y ou can all make your world a greener place
C ars are bad, walk to school!
L itter's bad so please don't throw it.
I n autumn, summer, winter and spring, recycle!
N ew compost is green
G et your green gloves on.

Alice May Briers (10)
Warton Nethersole's CE Primary School, Warton

Animals

Look after your animals.
Never keep them in cages.
Never keep them in handbags.
Never always keep them indoors.
Never always keep them outdoors.
Never give them too much food.
Never give them too little.
Never hurt animals.

Katie Harvey (9)
Warton Nethersole's CE Primary School, Warton

Animals

I like the animals
They are not criminals
They're good and should
Have you as a bud.
They are dying.

Harry White (10)
Warton Nethersole's CE Primary School, Warton

Make The World Nice

Don't litter, rubbish can kill,
For animals it's a death pill.
Turtles think they see a jellyfish,
But it's a bag that can kill, not a nice dish.
Otters and such get cut by cans,
Dropping litter should have a ban.
Plastic drink collars suffocate moles and mice,
Don't drop litter, make the world nice.

Louise Rose Greenhill (10)
Warton Nethersole's CE Primary School, Warton

Where Am I?

Why are people throwing food at me?
I like to hunt for my own food.
Why am I in a cage?
Why is there a chain and lock on my door?
I wish I was at home
With my mum, dad and friends.
I wish someone would take me home.
I am a monkey.

Matthew King (9)
Warton Nethersole's CE Primary School, Warton

Be Green

Hurry, hurry, save the environment today,
Do not drive to school!
Throw your car away today,
It will help the world.
Please do not pollute the world.
Do not be mean, be green!

Jayden Wood (10)
Warton Nethersole's CE Primary School, Warton

Recycle This, Recycle That

Recycle this paper
Recycle that bottle
Recycle that can
Put it in the bin
Help the world live
Help the world survive
Do you want a clean world?
Then help us to *recycle!*

Megan Allman (8)
Warton Nethersole's CE Primary School, Warton

Trapped Animals

Where am I?
I'm a monkey.
Why are people throwing food at me?
What are these metal things that are trapping me?
Where is my mum?
I want to get my own food.
I need to get out.
Please help me!

Dannie Price (8)
Warton Nethersole's CE Primary School, Warton

Don't Smoke

Whatever you do, don't smoke in cars,
Stinky, smelly smoke kills.
It damages your lungs.
Please don't smoke.
You get one minute off your life
Every time you smoke!

Liam Gardner (9)
Warton Nethersole's CE Primary School, Warton

Rubbish

My mum has lots of rubbish,
She puts it in the rubbish bin.
I say, 'No!'
She says, 'Why?'
I say, 'Please don't!
Pop it in this instead!'

Recycling really does matter.

Jack Mason (10)
Warton Nethersole's CE Primary School, Warton

Peaceful Freezing Land

As the wind blows in, out, things get cold and chilly
Seals dance and penguins flap
Peace is all around
All the animals dance and jump up and down
Everything is freezing and very, very cold
But it is peaceful to everybody

Let's keep it that way!

Michael Keeling (9)
Warton Nethersole's CE Primary School, Warton

Save Our Animals

A nimals are harmless creatures and they won't hurt you.
N asty people should stop poaching and killing them.
I n the jungle animals get killed by predators.
M ake people stop killing the animals for their skins.
A nimals are great fun to watch in the zoo.
L ots of people keep killing on purpose.
S ome people are nasty people and they should stop killing them.

Georgina Ann Hartop (7)
Warton Nethersole's CE Primary School, Warton

Go Green!

Go green!
Green as grass!
Do it now,
Make a difference to the world.
Icebergs falling, polluted, crashing, flooding.
That's what's ahead if we don't stop now.
And disease in a giant sneeze!

Jacob Sharratt (10)
Warton Nethersole's CE Primary School, Warton

Save Our Animals

A nimals are harmless creatures
N asty humans should stop poaching
I n the jungle there are fires, so stop it whoever you are!
M ean people can do lots of nasty stuff
A nimals can be very loud and scary at times
L iars can be caught when not expected
S ome people do not know how it feels to die. (Please help them!).

Olivia Hopkins
Warton Nethersole's CE Primary School, Warton

Save Our Animals

A nimals are harmless creatures
N asty humans should stop poaching
I t is a shocking sight
M en are horrid hunters
A nimals get killed by people on purpose
L ittle animals are in danger
S mall animals go into fires and they die.

Robyn Turner (7)
Warton Nethersole's CE Primary School, Warton

Creatures

A nimals are harmless creatures
N asty humans should stop killing animals
I should help some of the animals
M aybe I should put some animals in safari parks
A nimals sometimes need looking after
L izards can change colour to protect themselves.
S o why don't we start looking after animals today?

Izabella Daulman (7)
Warton Nethersole's CE Primary School, Warton

Save Our Animals

A nimals are harmless creatures
N asty people should stop poaching
I ll animals could die quicker than ever
M illions of animals die every year
A frican elephants die a lot, I think they're becoming extinct
L iving animals are lucky they are alive today
S uffocating animals will die soon. Somebody please help them.

Dayle Lucy Turner (8)
Warton Nethersole's CE Primary School, Warton

Save Our Animals

A nimals are good things.
N asty people kill them.
I ncredibly mean people are happy after they're dead.
M ammals are extinct.
A nimals are dead.
L ive no longer
S o sad.

Lauren Chapman (7)
Warton Nethersole's CE Primary School, Warton

Save Our Animals

A nimals are in danger around
N asty people are killing animals around
I n our country we need to save paper
M ammals are being killed so we have endangered animals
A nimals are harmless but even they are being killed
L ittle animals are the same, they need help too
S nakes need help too!

Tania Critchley (7)
Warton Nethersole's CE Primary School, Warton

Save Our Animals

A nimals are nearly dead
N asty humans should stop
I am so, so sad because nearly every animal is extinct
M ammals are becoming extinct
A nimals are harmless creatures
L iving creatures are lucky
S ome animals are extinct.

Georgia Ann Allbrighton (8)
Warton Nethersole's CE Primary School, Warton

Save Our Animals

A nimals are harmless creatures
N asty humans should stop poaching
I n the forests there are loads of trees and bushes
M onkeys climb from tree to tree
A nimals are living creatures
L et animals live forever
S top killing the animals!

Morgan Norris (8)
Warton Nethersole's CE Primary School, Warton

Save Our Animals

A nimals are harmless creatures
N asty people should be ashamed of themselves
I 'm sad for the creatures
M y friends are sad for them
A lligators are the scariest things ever
L ittle animals are cute
S nakes are the most harmless things ever.

Owen Collins (7)
Warton Nethersole's CE Primary School, Warton

Animals

A rchers should stop shooting
N asty people do it
I n forests
M ammals may be nice but nasty people kill
A rchers should go to jail
L osers they are, but we can save the animals
S o tell the Queen or the police now!

Jacob Wilson (7)
Warton Nethersole's CE Primary School, Warton

Rainforests

Don't let the rainforest die,
People say litter's OK but it's a lie.
There are animals in there,
Perhaps a never discovered bear.
The rainforest is a wonderful place,
Full of life but you might forget a familiar face.
Please recycle and make the world a better place.

Robbie Barker (10)
Warton Nethersole's CE Primary School, Warton

Save Our Animals

A nimals are harmless creatures
N asty humans should stop poaching
I ce shouldn't be melted in the North Pole
M ammals shouldn't be killed because they are precious
A im the gun, but don't shoot
L and is precious for animals
S mart people don't kill.

Ellie Humphries (7)
Warton Nethersole's CE Primary School, Warton

What Mummy Says

Don't throw litter into the sea,
Because my mummy says to me,
'It kills animals every day
Because of us throwing litter away.'
So because of what Mummy says,
Do not throw your litter away!

Harriet Critchley (10)
Warton Nethersole's CE Primary School, Warton

Save The Sea

Stop throwing litter in the sea,
Because it's just as bad as wasting electricity.
And if you throw a bag and lid,
You might kill a turtle or squid.
If you stop throwing litter today.
Then the manta ray will say, 'Hooray!'

Michael Cotterill (10)
Warton Nethersole's CE Primary School, Warton

Recycle, Recycle

Cycle, cycle down to the recycling plant,
Recycle, recycle is so relevant.
Too much garbage on the Earth,
See what garbage is worth.
Pollution is spreading fast,
It is going to the past.

Joshua Garfield (10)
Warton Nethersole's CE Primary School, Warton

Don't Do This

Please don't smoke,
Please recycle your rubbish,
Please don't kill endangered animals,
Please protect the environment.
Please, please!
Together with can save the world.

Cameron Adam (8)
Warton Nethersole's CE Primary School, Warton

Smoking Kills

Smoking kills, smoking smells, smoke is in the air.
Smoke makes your lungs go black and makes your teeth rot!
It makes you cough.
If you smoke when children are in the car, you poison them.
Please, please, stop smoking, help the environment, yourself
and your children.

Nicole (9) & Lizzy (8)
Warton Nethersole's CE Primary School, Warton

Litter

If you litter everyone will suffer.
The animals will eat the litter and die.
It will make our world look sad and grey.
So let's not litter and make it better.

Isabelle Hounsome (10)
Warton Nethersole's CE Primary School, Warton

Save The Deep Blue Sea

I know some of you are bitter,
That doesn't mean you can drop your litter,
In the big blue sea,
Where animals swim free!

Eleanor Crowley (10)
Warton Nethersole's CE Primary School, Warton

Recycle

Recycle, recycle don't let the world die.
Recycle, recycle the people will die.
Recycle, recycle make the world green.
Recycle, recycle we will survive.

Jaremi Rubin (12)
Warton Nethersole's CE Primary School, Warton

Being Green

B eing green is not all that clean
E veryone try and be green
I n all of us there is something green
N ow get down on your hands and knees
G o on, I dare you to try and be green.

G irls and boys, young and old, try and be green
R eady, steady, give it a go, it takes time so no rushing
E veryone just try
E veryone, you know what to do
N ow you've heard, just do it!

Chloe-Louise Storer (11)
Westways Primary School, Sheffield

Healthy Planet

H ow can you help our planet?
E verybody can do their part.
A lways put rubbish in bins.
L ook after endangered animals.
T ake care of your planet.
H elp to recycle.
Y ou can make a difference if you try.

P ut a bit of effort in, it will really make a difference.
L et's get moving everyone.
A t last it has finished.
N ow we're officially done.
E veryone be happy
T reat yourself.

Eleanor Marlow (7)
Whitwick St John the Baptist CE Primary School, Coalville

Endangered

E co-kids can change the world and make it a better place
N asty, naughty bacteria and germs make the planet a disgrace.
D anger, animals are losing their habitats. Can we find them
a new place?
A ngry adults aren't making the world a better place, now it's a disgrace.
N aughty people don't help at all. If you look everywhere there's
garbage from them all.
G reat litter pickers help the world become a cleaner place. Why
don't you try and help and put it in its place?
E xtremely intelligent children help the country too. They make this
planet better, can you?
R ecycling helps everyone. I help too. There's one more thing I
need to tell you, you can help too!
E xcellent litter pickers make the world great. If you find any put
it in its place.
D angerous rainforests are getting chopped down, if we can't
stop them can you?

Abbie Harmer (8)
Whitwick St John the Baptist CE Primary School, Coalville

Bitter Litter

If I see you drop litter
It makes me feel bitter.
Please put your litter in the bin.

If you want to feel fantastic!
Recycle all your plastic!
Cardboard, glass and tin.

If we all work together
We'll make it forever
A better place to live.

Ellie Harman (7)
Whitwick St John the Baptist CE Primary School, Coalville

Litter

Please keep our world clean,
Cos it's in a state.
I don't want to be mean,
But please keep our world clean.
Put litter in the bins,
Tidy away your mess,
Paper, glass, food and tins,
All need to go in the bins.
It's up to us to keep it clean,
So don't forget the rules,
Use it, don't drop it, find a bin,
To help keep our world clean.

Ellie Olivia Oldham (8)
Whitwick St John the Baptist CE Primary School, Coalville

A Better World

Imagine a world with no waste,
A world where nothing was thrown away in haste,
A world where everyone wants to save,
A planet that God once gave.
Reuse, recycle, so easy to say,
But we must do this each and every day.
So let's make our world the best place to live,
All it takes is for us to give,
Some time, some love,
Some thought, some care
Because we always want our world to be there.

Kieran Joshua Nutting (7)
Whitwick St John the Baptist CE Primary School, Coalville

Pollution

P lease stop and think about
O ur eco-community's global pout
L isten to me and you will see
L eads to a better life
U nderstand that driving cars
T here and there again
I s going to end up killing you and me
O ur children will lead a poorer life
N ever being happy, instead they will live in strife.

Dominic Leake (9)
Whitwick St John the Baptist CE Primary School, Coalville

The World

T he world is a wonderful place.
H elp us clean up after our mess.
E veryone should help our environment.

W hy do we allow it to get in such a state?
O n our streets there's rubbish everywhere.
R ubbish is supposed to be in bins not on the streets.
L ook after our community.
D rop your litter in the bin and the world will be much cleaner.

Carleigh Attwal (9)
Whitwick St John the Baptist CE Primary School, Coalville

Litter

L itter, litter everywhere
I sn't it a mess!
T idy up and pick it up.
T he world would be a better place if
E verybody did their bit
R ecycle, recycle, recycle.

Megan Riley (7)
Whitwick St John the Baptist CE Primary School, Coalville

Beaches And Seas

On beaches and in seas, cans and bottles, they're everywhere.
Why don't you help clean the beaches and seas?
See how well you can do it!
I've never had a go but I would like to soon.
Paper, bottles, cans and plastic.
Pick them up and that's all you have to do!

Leah Grace Sibson (7)
Whitwick St John the Baptist CE Primary School, Coalville

Rubbish

Litter, litter everywhere.
People dropping it
Just don't care.
If they drop it in their houses
One day the world
Will be full of little mice.

Alice Wilson (9)
Whitwick St John the Baptist CE Primary School, Coalville

Litter

L ots of rubbish all around.
I s this what we want to see?
T ake your rubbish home with you!
T idy up your mess!
E nvironmentally friendly is what we need to be.
R emember, put it in the bin!

Abbie Acton (8)
Whitwick St John the Baptist CE Primary School, Coalville

Save The Environment

Pick up your litter if you drop it.
To save:
Plants, birds and mammals, from their death.
The world will be polluted if you keep dropping litter.
Care about the environment;
Save it from being polluted.

Abigail Munro (8)
Whitwick St John the Baptist CE Primary School, Coalville

Untitled

Litter, litter spend it, lend it,
What would it be next?
Litter, litter flies around
The world getting recycled.
Litter, litter one person's rubbish
Is another person's gift.

Libby Keeling (7)
Whitwick St John the Baptist CE Primary School, Coalville

What To Do?

It's time to think what to do.
The ice caps are melting, you know what to do.
Stop using the cars, that's what to do.
Help the environment, you know what to do.
Just do what you can do.
Please!

Emelia Jade Elton (9)
Whitwick St John the Baptist CE Primary School, Coalville

Just One World

G reenhouse gases are bad.
R ecycling nothing would be mad.
E ating healthily, we really should.
E nergy-saving light bulbs are good.
N o more pollution - it makes me sad!

Daniel Ward (8)
Whitwick St John the Baptist CE Primary School, Coalville

Rubbish Issues

Rubbish is a bad thing to drop,
It will make more mess.

So do not drop cans or glass,
Or any other rubbish.

There are many bins around,
So put your rubbish in them.

So help the environment more,
By putting it in the bin
And not on the floor!

Sammy Jarvis-Evans
Ysgol Glan Conwy, Colwyn Bay

How To Help Global Warming

Stop causing the world pain
With your cars and aeroplanes.

There are some things you can do,
To make it better and start anew.

Don't go in the car if you're not in a rush,
Walk, run or go on the bus.

Don't throw rubbish on the floor,
Recycle! Don't make it feel like a chore.

These are some things you can do.
So walk, run, go on the bus and recycle too!

Jonathon Coates (10)
Ysgol Glan Conwy, Colwyn Bay

Save The World

Help the world survive
So we all can stay alive.
Turn off the lights
During the night.
Recycle lots of plastic
That will be fantastic.
Recycle! Energy-saving lights will do
Buy a set of two.
Try your very best
So the world can have a rest.

Owen Parmley (10)
Ysgol Glan Conwy, Colwyn Bay

Global Warming

The planet is getting hot
The greenhouse effect, that's what!
It's not that easy to spot.

There is more grey than green
Everywhere it is seen
It's not the best sight you can see.

We will need to recycle and save energy,
If you do that you will soon see
That the planet will be saved for you and me!

Charlotte Wright (10)
Ysgol Glan Conwy, Colwyn Bay

Saving Energy

Saving energy is the best
Turn things off and give them a rest!

Don't boil the kettle and let it go cold,
Stay there are wait like you're told!

Turn off the lights when it's night
Don't waste energy when it's bright.

Put the energy-saving lights in your rooms,
It will save money and it won't end in doom.

Becky Jarvis-Evans
Ysgol Glan Conwy, Colwyn Bay

Young Writers Information

We hope you have enjoyed reading this book - and that you will continue to enjoy it in the coming years.

If you like reading and writing poetry drop us a line, or give us a call, and we'll send you a free information pack.

Alternatively if you would like to order further copies of this book or any of our other titles, then please give us a call or log onto our website at www.youngwriters.co.uk

Young Writers Information
Remus House
Coltsfoot Drive
Peterborough
PE2 9JX
(01733) 890066